Until You See Me

Ellen Eve

Copyright © Ellen Eve 2022

All rights reserved.

ISBN: 9798356264542

"We are most alive when we are in love."

CONTENTS

	Acknowledgments	i
1	Chapter	1
2	Chapter	10
3	Chapter	15
4	Chapter	24
5	Chapter	46
6	Chapter	56
7	Chapter	60
8	Chapter	70
9	Chapter	82
10	Chapter	100
11	Chapter	106
12	Chapter	117
13	Chapter	126
14	Chapter	132
15	Chapter	143
16	Chapter	147
17	Chapter	153
18	Chapter	161
19	Chapter	168
20	Chapter	173

21	Chapter	184
	Epilogue	194

This is a work of fiction. Names, characters, businesses, organizations, places, events and incidents either are the product of the author' imagination or are used fictitiously. Any resemblance to actual persons, living or dead, events, or locales is entirely coincidental.

1 CHAPTER

Melissa's phone rang in her pocket as she hurried up the steps to her apartment carrying groceries in both hands. She fished around for her keys inside her handbag and dropped the bags at the entrance, leaving the door open.

"Hello?"

"Well, it's about time, Mandy. What took you so long? I've called million times!"

Melissa rolled her eyes. Exaggeration was one of her mother's talents. "Good morning, Mum. I hope you are well. I received literally two calls from you whilst walking up the stairs."

"Well, it *felt* like ages. Especially since I have something to tell you."

Melissa pushed the door shut and supported the phone against her shoulder to carry the shopping in the small kitchenette. "What is it, Mum?"

"Patrick is dead."

Melissa froze. "What?"

"You remember Patrick? He was part of the cricket team and the best friend of the Ferrero twins. Her mother and I went to the same middle school."

Melissa relaxed. "Yes, I think I can vaguely recall seeing him once or twice whilst growing up."

"Well, he is dead now," her mother blurted, and loud sobs filled the speaker.

Melissa sighed. "Jeez, Mum. I'm so sorry to hear. Please don't cry. I didn't know you were close to his family. Last time I checked, you and Ophelia weren't speaking."

"Well, during a time like this, I believe their family need all the support they can get."

Melissa nodded and unpacked her shopping. "Absolutely, Mum. You are right."

"So, can I count on your full support as well?"

"Of course, whatever you need."

The moment the words slipped from Melissa's mouth, she could have kicked herself.

"That's great, Mandy. I'll expect you to be here this weekend to escort me to the funeral. I don't want to go alone."

"Oh, Mum. I don't know. I didn't know him at all and haven't seen him since I left Canford Cliffs. Besides, I already had the weekend off last month for..." Melissa paused. "For Dad's funeral."

"I know, Mandy, but surely you wouldn't want to send me to the funeral alone."

Melissa had to agree with her mother. She had been shattered and unable to eat for days when her father had an early heart attack, which no one had expected.

"Well, I guess I can come down to Canford Cliffs, but I need to leave with the first train on Monday morning without fail. I mean it, I've taken too many long weekends lately."

"Great, honey. Will you stay at a hotel in the city centre, or would you like to stay with me?"

"No, Mum. I will stay at Dad's old house where I've always stayed when I'm in town."

"Well, suit yourself. I don't know what you see in that old log house anyway."

"It's called memories."

"I prefer to look at the future instead of living in the past. I'll see you on Friday!"

"Hold on, wait, Mum!" Melissa yelled, but her mother had already ended the call.

Melissa dropped the phone onto the kitchen counter and finished unpacking.

She wasn't enthusiastic to return to Canford Cliffs so soon after her father's passing. She had barely survived the funeral and already dreaded the weekend, but she didn't want to fail her mother. After all, she was the only relative she had left.

***

Melissa arrived early on Friday morning at Canford Cliffs.

She dropped off her weekender at her father's house and opened the thick curtains to allow natural light to enter the house. She inhaled the ocean breeze and changed into the same black dress and pumps she had worn to her father's funeral, which she matched with a blazer and a silk scarf. She left her hair loose and applied red lipstick to draw people's attention away from the dark circles under her eyes.

Her father's spiritual presence in the house brought her comfort, but it only made his absence even worse. Melissa partly expected to see him in the backyard tending to his precious plants, but she would never have the pleasure of witnessing his passion again. A lump formed in her throat, and she turned to check her reflection in the entrance mirror before heading to the rental car outside.

Melissa arrived at the address her mother had texted her earlier that day and spotted her waiting in the parking lot.

"You're late."

"I don't think so. You said three o'clock and here I am."

Her mother crossed her hands and pursed her lip. "I wanted to arrive early to mingle before the service. "

"Mum, this is someone's funeral. I don't think it's an appropriate place to *mingle*."

Melissa sighed and followed her mother to the entrance.

The funeral was a far cry from a traditional English one. The walls of the old county hall were covered with photos of Patrick and the tables were full of treats, which had been moved aside in a U-shape so people could talk with each other.

"Mum, you didn't tell me it was going to be the event of the year. I don't know half of these people," Melissa whispered as she smiled at the young couple passing by.

"It must have slipped my mind," her mother responded and hurried over to the grieving family who were welcoming the guests at the entrance.

Melissa followed, eyeing her mother's floral dress that was everything else but suitable for a funeral.

Her mother threw herself into a tight embrace. "My darling, I'm so sorry for your loss, it's horrible what happened. I still can't believe it!"

"My deep condolences for your loss Mr and Mrs Reed," Melissa said and suddenly realised she had no idea what had happened to Patrick.

They left the grieving family and followed the crowd. "Mum, what happened to Patrick?"

"Mandy, you don't know?"

Melissa rolled her eyes. "If I did, I wouldn't be asking."

Her mother's eyes lit as she scanned the room to ensure that no one was listening and lowered her voice. "Car accident. Apparently, Patrick had been drinking with one of the Ferrero twins and they never made it home."

"Oh my god, that's terrible!" Melissa replied, feeling for his parents.

Patrick had only been a couple of years older than her, and the apple of their eyes.

Her mother nodded. "It was horrible, I saw the car on local news. They crashed with a lorry."

"But who drove the car?" Melissa asked, but her question was left unanswered when her mother became surrounded by her friends.

"Pick up something to eat, Mandy, and enjoy the party!" her mother said and sailed away.

Melissa felt mortified by her mother's untactful attitude and wanted to remind her that the 'party' she referred to was someone's funeral, but her mother was long gone by the time she had opened her mouth to speak. Melissa sighed again and made her way to the tables.

She tried to decide between duck liver pâté and pigs in blankets when someone lightly tugged on the hem of her black blazer. She turned around and gazed two feet down into a pair of hazel eyes staring at her from a wheelchair.

If Melissa had wondered what had happened to the other passengers in the car, she didn't have to anymore as she stood face-to-face with Andres Ferrero.

He was still a handsome man with Hispanic heritage, received from his late mother. He had straight black hair and playful hazel eyes with a sleek, freshly shaven face. He wore a designer suit and shiny leather shoes, which poked out underneath the dark green blanket that covered his legs.

"Melissa Cunnington, I didn't expect to see you here. It's been a long time. How are you?"

Melissa remained quiet and observed the man in front of her.

During their childhood, she had been lucky if Andres, the captain of the cricket team and the local millionaire thanks to their father's agriculture empire, had spoken more than two words to her.

Andres tilted his head. "Are you going to react at all or just stare at me?"

Melissa recovered quickly. "Hi, Andres… it's good to see you," she muttered and held out her hand.

Andres took it but instead of shaking it, he caressed the sensitive part of her wrist and kissed her palm. "Trust me, the pleasure is all mine."

He smiled and Melissa pulled her hand back. She turned to fill her plate with food, but Andres grabbed the plate from Melissa's hand.

"Allow me," he said. "Can I make you the Andres' special?"

Melissa had no idea what he meant but smiled and nodded, the shock stopping her from speaking.

Andres chatted lightly whilst filling up Melissa's plate with an assortment of food before he turned and did the same for himself.

"Thanks, Andres, this is very kind of you. Anyway, I'm great! How are you?" Melissa said, but she quickly realised the awkwardness of her question. "Oh, sorry. I didn't mean to obtrude!"

Andres took two glasses of champagne and motioned for her to move aside from the tables. "I guess you meant to ask what happened to me?"

"No, no, not at all!"

"It's ok. It's no secret that it was me who was with Patrick in the car when he died. The crash threw him right through the glass, so he died immediately, but I got stuck in the car and damaged my legs."

Melissa gasped. "I'm so sorry to hear."

Andres shrugged. "Happens to the best of us."

"But you find yourself in good health considering the circumstances?"

"You could say so."

They chatted for a while until Melissa excused herself to find her mother. She enjoyed small talk now and then but seeing Andres like this sent chills down her spine.

"Do you really have to go?" Andres asked.

"I'm afraid I do, I need to find my mum and get her home."

"Well, let me at least offer you dinner tomorrow night at my house for old-time's sake. Let's say… 8 o' clock?"

Melissa raised her eyebrows with surprise. She didn't recall any 'old times' with him at all. In fact, both of Sir Daniel's offspring had spent most of their lives in private schools and then went travelling.

"Wow, Andres, thank you for your very kind invitation, but I don't think I will have time as I'm here only until Monday morning and…"

But before Melissa had the chance to politely decline his invitation, her mother interrupted their conversation.

"*Darling*, of course you have time for it. It's only Friday evening and you have all of tomorrow and Sunday before you return to London on Monday," she chirped.

Melissa tried to hide her annoyance but was too polite to overrule her mother's obvious match-making attempt.

"Well, I guess I could make myself available for tomorrow night," Melissa mumbled.

"That's great! I'll see you tomorrow at 8 o'clock, then?"

"You definitely will!" Melissa's mother replied with a smile.

Andres beamed and wheeled himself towards the exit. Melissa returned the smile and headed outside the county hall, her mother following her to the rental car.

"Oh my *God*, this is something, Mandy! Do you know what this means?"

"I've dated men before, Mum, this shouldn't be any different."

Her mother was barely able to hold on to her seat. "Think about it, Mandy. The endless possibilities when dating a man as powerful as Andres Ferrero."

Melissa grinned. "As far as I recall, his older brother still runs the main business."

Her mother glared at her. "Hugo? He hasn't shown his face here for a long time. Besides, you can't get two words out of that man. You're much better off with someone charming like Andres."

The memory of Hugo still gave Melissa goosebumps. He might have been only three minutes older than his brother, but he had imposed silent respect with his calm, observing character that had left many locals feeling uneasy.

"I don't know, Mum. I don't want to lead people on, especially since I have no interest in pursuing a relationship."

"Rubbish, of course you are interested! He is the most eligible bachelor in the country, and now he is in a wheelchair, he is clearly considering someone humble instead of all the models he used to date back in London."

Melissa rolled her eyes at her mother's untactful comment, which wasn't the first. "Jeez, Mum, thanks. I didn't know you considered me that dull."

***

Melissa stopped in front of her mother's town house in the city centre of Canford Cliffs, only a couple of miles from her late father's house.

After their divorce, her mother had insisted on renting a flat in the centre of the small city despite the plenty of room they had in her father's house, even for a separated couple.

She helped her mother out of the car and inside the building.

"Mandy, I strongly think you should stop playing around and leave that comfort zone of yours. Think about your future; this might be your lucky chance," her mother said, and strategically paused between her words. "Your father and I talked about it many times, you know. He was so worried about your future and scared of you ending up alone."

Melissa ignored the flash of pain as she thought about her father and kissed the air on either side of her mother's cheeks.

"Goodnight, Mum," she replied.

Melissa returned to her, full of frustration, and turned car the steering wheel towards her father's house.

My mother truly knows how to push my buttons after all these years, she thought as she parked outside her father's house and rested her forehead on the cold steering wheel, calming down. A lonely, melancholic tear emerged from the corner of her eye, but she wiped it away and dragged herself inside and up to her old bedroom, grateful that her father had kept it the same until the day he had died.

2 CHAPTER

Hugo waited outside and watched his brother emerge from the main entrance of the county hall. He opened the door of the black Range Rover.

"Do you need a hand, brother?" Hugo said, offering his hand.

"Get your hands away from me, like you haven't done enough!" Andres barked, and with the support of his upper body, he pulled himself onto the back seat of the car.

Hugo pressed his lips together as he folded the wheelchair and lifted it into the back. He returned to the driver's seat when two women walking through the parking lot caught his eye. He immediately recognised Laura Cunnington, who had become quite a town celebrity following her divorce, but he had to rub his eyes again when he saw the woman next to her.

The woman's golden locks were exactly like her mother's, but she had inherited her icy blue eyes from her late father. Just like a tiger eying its prey, Hugo found himself lost in the sway of her hips as she strutted in high heels. He watched her open the door for her mother and then walk around her car. He held his breath when the black dress ran up her thighs and stretched around her bum as she sat behind the steering wheel.

"I couldn't believe my eyes either when I saw her today at the funeral. She has changed," Andres said from behind him.

Hugo broke his stare and powered the engine. "Okay? I didn't even notice."

"Of course you did. I could see it miles away. Too bad she is only the heiress of the shitty log house her father built to impress her cheap mother once upon a time. With our looks, you could do so much better."

"I'm not interested." Hugo shrugged, but his brother's words stuck in his mind.

With his athletic, 6'2-foot body and Hispanic heritage, he had never had trouble awakening the interest of the opposite sex. On the contrary, his brother had taken full advantage of the exotic appearance that had given them charm and mystery since they were teenagers. His brother swept women off their feet more than Hugo could remember, often to the extent that he usually found sanctuary at the local library or the forest surrounding the Ferrero estate.

Considering the time he had spent in the forests during his childhood, it was no wonder that he had ended up roaming the foreign lands to look for new product lines for his father's ever-growing multi-billion empire.

"I don't know if I should feel relieved that you find her attractive now. Back in the day, I remember you checking out her small tits and boyish frame more than I'd like to remember."

Hugo turned and swung his fist at him, but Andres still had the instincts of the ex-captain of the cricket team, dodging just in time and glaring at him with rage.

"You think that's funny? I've been discharged from the hospital literally last week and I've lost my ability to walk. What's wrong with you?"

He was right.

"Cut the crap, Andres. Let's go."

Hugo huffed through gritted teeth and backed out of the parking lot before sinking into his thoughts again.

Andres hadn't been completely wrong. Coincidentally, it was at the local library where Hugo had first set eyes on Melissa as a young girl. It hadn't been the boyish figure he had been after, but the peace and quietness that had surrounded her. Just the medicine Hugo had been looking for after losing his mother.

There was nothing boyish about her now, Hugo thought and let the small Fiat Punto push into the car park. She couldn't see him through the darkened front glass, which offered Hugo an opportunity to watch her bite her lower lip as she drove the narrow exit.

"Well, since you *obviously* have zero interest in her, I hope you don't mind that I asked her for dinner tomorrow night at the mansion?"

Hugo's first instinct was to punch his brother, but his vulnerable stage stopped him and instead, he remained silent as he manoeuvred the car outside the parking lot.

"I don't care what you do, Brother. You want to ask her out, do it. You want to fuck her, do that as well."

Ignoring his brother's words, Andres leaned back in the seat.

"I might since she accepted my invitation without a struggle. On the contrary, she seemed to be quite excited about it. *Desperate* even," he mocked, tabbing his legs.

Hugo glanced at him from the interior mirror. "There is nothing funny about your medical condition. You should be happy to be alive."

Andres's face darkened. "And whose fault is that, Brother? Who condemned me to this chair for the rest of my life?"

Andres' words hurt, especially as Hugo had driven the car on the night of the accident.

"It doesn't matter, we have more important things to consider, such as getting you up to speed with your physio. The doctor said there still might be a chance you could walk."

"Right, walking with crutches or other aids like Grandpa, but I will never run or play cricket again. Shoot me now, please."

"On the contrary, Brother, you have been given a second chance in life, don't waste it."

"It's easy for you to say. How I wish it was you in that passenger seat instead of me, maybe you would stop being a dickhead!"

"Well, we would have all died in a blink of an eye because you were drunk on that night and in no condition to drive," Hugo said and parked the car near the front entrance of the Ferrero mansion.

"Shall I get the nurse out to help you?" Hugo asked, eyeing the recently added ramp on the side of the stairs.

"Well, I can't possibly get up myself, can I?"

Hugo made a quick call, and after a short while, a nurse appeared from inside. "You should consider hiring permanent help. The nurses can't work from the house forever."

"I would but I can't work anymore, and I've got no money for it," Andres complained.

Hugo sighed. "Andres, you know you haven't worked a day in your life. Your monthly allowance has been more than enough to cover all your costs and impulse purchases."

"Well, even if I *wanted* to work, it's too late for me now. Plus, my monthly allowance is not enough to look after this house and hire help."

"Right, I'll have a look at the finances tomorrow and make necessary adjustments to your allowance," Hugo said and returned to the car. "But you should know, many people work in your condition and live a happy life. Why don't you change your attitude? I don't know, start working out, get married and stuff."

"Sure, I'll make a note to suggest that to Melissa tomorrow during our romantic night together."

Hugo tightened his crib on the car door until his knuckles whitened and his face turned red, but he swallowed his rage. There was no point arguing with his brother.

"Do whatever you find it necessary, Brother. Good night," Hugo said and disappeared behind the steering wheel.

On the way to the main motorway, Hugo let his mind wander. He knew that his brother's mean, self-deprecating jokes attempted to cover his pain, and in any other circumstances, he would have tried to console him, but Andres' sulky attitude had always kept their relationship distant.

We might look the same, but our lives couldn't be more apart, Hugo thought as his mind wandered to Andres' words about Melissa.

Melissa

Andres' joke about her wouldn't have had the impact it did if she had declined his dinner invitation, which would have made sense since Melissa had never shown any interest in either of them, but something had clearly changed.

My unstable brother and the self-confident Melissa couldn't possibly be a good combination, especially since there was something in her icy blue eyes that could trap a man in a heartbeat, Hugo thought and took the exit from the motorway.

London would have to wait.

3 CHAPTER

In the comfort of her bedroom, Melissa peeled off her black dress and sighed with relief; her body could breathe, and she could now move around freely.

She changed into an oversized jumper and leggings and slid her feet into her leather slides. Her mother's words still haunted her mind as she let the sharp stabs of pain flush over her in the comfort of her father's house.

At the age of twenty-eight, she didn't consider herself old, yet most of her friends from the small town had married young, which wasn't uncommon, especially in small towns outside the influence of the capital where the average age of building a family had quickly spiked in the recent decade. Many women not only decided to gain more independence and put more emphasis on their careers, but they also considered the increasing cost of living, not to mention the astronomical rental market.

Who in their right mind would even consider starting a family in their late 20s? Melissa wondered.

Moreover, Melissa was almost convinced that her mother was lying about her father worrying about her future, but since her father could no longer defend himself, a seed of doubt entered her mind as she made her way back downstairs. It wasn't enough having lost her father not long ago, but second-guessing his last thoughts ticked on her temples, causing her neck to stiffen and ache. She gently massaged her neck as she entered the kitchen to prepare a cup of chamomile tea.

As Melissa let the teabag brew, she replayed her father's fears in her mind. She had never discussed her future with him...but he had never brought it up with her either. Could he have been worrying in secret all along? Could her mother be right for once?

While Melissa continued to question everything, the doorbell interrupted her train of thought.

Melissa glanced at the clock on the kitchen wall and frowned; 11:45 was *not* the time to turn up at someone's house unannounced.

The doorbell chimed again, and Melissa tiptoed through the hallway towards the front door. She peered through the entrance window to see the silhouette of a tall figure on the other side.

"Who is it?" she hooted, holding the doorknob.

The unknown visitor remained silent, but suddenly rattled the handle as if to try and get inside.

Melissa jumped back and her heart pounded with terror.

"If you don't reveal your identity, you will leave me no choice but to call the police!" Melissa barked, afraid that no one would notice her disappearance if the mysterious person had ill intentions.

The doorknob stopped moving and the entrance remained silent. The lack of response made the hair on her neck stand on end and goosebumps covered her skin.

Melissa cleared her throat and loaded her husky voice with authority. "I mean it, the town is not that big, the police will be here in minutes!"

Her loose threat seemed to have worked as the person paused and turned away from the door. The sound of their footsteps faded, and she relaxed her shoulders and exhaled.

Melissa relaxed. She had gotten used to people mixing up her apartment with someone else's in her cramped London building but mistaking an entire house in such a small town surprised her.

She brushed off the strange encounter and returned to the kitchen when she bumped into a strong chest. A pair of muscular arms grabbed her, and her instinct told her to fight.

"Let me go! Keep your hands off me!" Melissa screamed, kicking the intruder to his knees.

She stepped back and whipped her hair away from her face. "I swear to God, you will not get away with this!"

The man's arms loosened from around her and a husky voice spoke. "Melissa, isn't it?"

Melissa stared at the tall figure before her, and her eyes met a familiar face.

"Andres—" Melissa guessed, but she covered her mouth with embarrassment when she realised that the man who *stood* in her house couldn't possibly be Andres.

Hugo shook his head and a sarcastic smile appeared on his face. "Think again, *Mona-Lisa*. I believe you met my brother earlier today, so you should be well-informed of his medical condition."

"Oh, I didn't mean that... I'm so sorry," Melissa apologised, but she paused and dipped her brow.

She stepped back and crossed her hands over her chest. "I mean, what are you doing here breaking into people's homes?"

With confidence, Andres's twin brother moved her aside like a doll and stepped inside the small kitchen. Melissa scoffed with incredulousness and waited for his explanation.

"I saw a strange car in the driveway and decided to check that no one planned to rob the place. Your father's death headlined the news, so naturally, people with ill intentions would assume the house is empty," Hugo said, curiously eying Melissa's steaming teacup.

For a second, Melissa wanted to grab her teacup from the kitchen counter and cover his arrogant face in hot liquid, but she kept her cool.

"Well, as you now know, the car is mine. I rented it when I arrived," Melissa explained, tightening her unsupported chest.

Suddenly, she was very conscious of not wearing a bra underneath her jumper, as she hadn't expected any visitors at this hour.

"I see you arrived at Patrick's memorial service like everyone else," Hugo said.

He opened one of the kitchen cupboards and grabbed a teacup and a pack of tea biscuits from the top shelf.

Melissa opened her arms to stop him, but her braless breasts slumped under her jumper, causing her to close her arms to conceal them. The rough fabric rubbed against her sensitive skin, and she felt her nipples harden.

"Excuse me, what are you doing, Mr Ferrero?"

Although the arrogant prick shared blood with Andres, he hadn't been such a familiar face in the town compared to his brother. In fact, Melissa could only remember crossing paths with him once or twice before he disappeared.

"Just Hugo," he said, pouring hot water into his cup. "I'm sure you are on a first-name basis with my brother as well."

Melissa scowled at Hugo and pursed her lips in frustration.

"And just to let you know, I've seen your nipples through your jumper since you bumped into me, so there is no reason to be shy now, just relax."

Melissa gasped. "For goodness's sake!"

Melissa fled from the kitchen and raced upstairs to the sound of his masculine laughter. She stormed into her old bedroom and grabbed the simple, lace bra from her bed, glaring at the door to make sure Hugo didn't barge in while she changed. His arrogance infuriated her, but she couldn't help the goosebumps creep from under her skin when she felt the faint hint of his cologne following her in the air.

Melissa took a deep breath to calm the butterflies in her stomach and returned to the kitchen a few minutes later.

Hugo sat at the kitchen table, drinking his tea and scoffing the last pack of biscuits in the house as he flicked through the Financial Times.

"You got that from my handbag!" Melissa barked, pointing at the newspaper spread out before him. "How dare you go through my things!"

Hugo rolled his eyes. "Calm down, it's not like I had to rifle through your bag to get it."

Melissa huffed and crossed her arms. "You never answered my question – what are you doing here?"

"I told you, I thought someone planned to rob the house," Hugo repeated, lifting his gaze from the newspaper.

Hugo's presence overpowered the small room and Melissa's body tensed with unease. He let his eyes rest on her for a while before he returned his gaze to the newspaper, licked his thumb and forefinger and turned the next page. Melissa blushed at his intimate gesture, but she cleared her throat and tried to match his authoritative tone.

"I appreciate your concern, but now you know it's me, the *legal* owner of the property, you need to leave. It's late and I have to get up early tomorrow."

Hugo closed the newspaper and folded it neatly on the table. "I'm sure it won't take all day tomorrow to get ready for a date night with my brother. Besides, your old man said I would be welcome here anytime."

Melissa jerked her head back up and glowered at him. "How do you know I have a date with your brother?"

Hugo munched the last biscuit and used the colourful napkin on the table to wipe his mouth. "My brother told me."

"Um, okay?"

Melissa touched her neck nervously.

I don't want to get caught in the middle of a delicate family matter, she thought silently and wondered if she should call off the evening with Andres.

"Oh dear, indeed," Hugo said and directed his sharp look at her. "Why are you going out with my brother, anyway? I don't recall you showing much interest in any of us ten years back."

His rightful accusation brought Melissa back in time.

Canford Cliffs had been a peaceful place to live, but she had never felt connected to the local children. She had always considered herself a lonely wolf and enjoyed reading more than participating in local activities. In fact, one of her best memories included wandering to the windy beach close to her home. Usually, it hadn't taken her long to find a secure spot before sitting down and sinking her feet deep into the warm sand. Solemnly, a good book, the waves hitting the shore and the whistling wind were enough to accompany her.

She had stayed in Canford Cliffs until the day she received her acceptance letter to the University of Kent to study finance and accounting, which had offered her a way to leave Canford Cliffs without guilt or regret.

The university had been only hours away, allowing her to visit her parents every weekend just in time to witness their cracking marriage. She had always tried to stay neutral and never take sides whilst her parents were arguing, but she couldn't help feeling sorry for her father who had given all his life to her and her mother.

"Are you done daydreaming, or shall I give you another minute for you to reply to my simple question?"

Melissa blinked herself back to reality and desperately tried to remember his question.

"Well, your brother took me by surprise, and my mother thought it would be a good idea considering I haven't—"

"Do you always do what your mother says?" Hugo interrupted, striding towards her.

Melissa felt light-headed as Hugo's musky scent surrounded her, and she stole a moment to admire his black jeans and leather jacket that covered his muscular frame. She stared into his eyes and furrowed her brow.

"Your eyes are nearly black, not hazel," she mumbled as his warmth entered her joints.

Hugo laughed and inspected her features. "Thanks for the detailed description, I'll make a note of that."

"Oh no, I didn't mean it like that! I just meant… you are twins, but your brother's eyes are hazel, yours are more —"

"Whilst I appreciate your smart observation, the twin jokes are a little old now and I don't consider them entertaining whatsoever."

Melissa blushed and stepped away from him, her brain turning to mush, which was unusual as she worked with male colleagues every day. Why would Andres's brother be any different?

"Why would my father allow you to enter his house?" Melissa questioned, changing the topic.

"Because I kept him company when his only daughter, his *little Lizzy*, abandoned him for a big career in London," Hugo jabbed.

Melissa's eyes welled with tears at the sound of the old nickname her father had once given her, but she forced them back and glared at Hugo.

"It's hardly abandonment to live in a different city from your parents!" Melissa defended. "Besides, I visited them nearly every weekend and during the holidays."

Hugo tilted his head and smirked. "I'm sure that's exactly what your father thought on all those lonely nights with only the tick of the clock to keep him company."

Melissa's eyes sharpened. "How dare you guilt-trip me for my choices! We live in the 21st century, women have careers now *and* they run businesses. It shouldn't be a surprise to you."

Hugo's cocky smile disappeared, and his tone changed. "I didn't question your choices. I just pointed out that your father wasn't well for a long time before his heart attack, so he could have used more help around the house."

Two lonely tears emerged from the corners of Melissa's eyes as her stomach twisted with guilt. "You're lying."

Hugo lifted his hand towards Melissa's face and wiped the tears from her cheeks. "Now, what's the point in lying to someone I don't care about?"

Hugo's harsh words filled Melissa with an icy bitterness, but she refused to stoop to his level.

She narrowed her eyes and glared at him. "You need to go now."

Hugo dropped his hands back to his sides and nodded. "Easy, just cancel the date with my brother and you'll never hear from me again."

Melissa scoffed in disbelief. "Why should I cancel? I promised my mother I would go!"

Hugo huffed in frustration. "In that case, what would you do if your mother told you to do this?"

Melissa frowned, but before she could respond, Hugo pressed his warm lips against hers with such intensity that she had to grab his arms to maintain her balance. She tried to pull away from him but Hugo wrapped his muscular arms around her waist and yanked her closer. His lips tasted of chamomile tea and sweet biscuits, and his fierce passion sent her into a moment of pure bliss. Heat surged down Melissa's body and her stomach swirled with butterflies as electric passion continued to fill the kitchen.

Melissa lost herself in his embrace when Hugo suddenly pushed her away. He wiped his mouth and grimaced as if he had been forced to kiss her.

"Well, it looks like you *are* mummy's girl after all," Hugo mocked. "Your father would be thrilled to know how you entertain strangers in his house. *Even though*, it's the 21st century, as you stated."

Melissa opened her mouth to speak, but the combination of breathlessness and speechlessness overwhelmed her. Her lips burned from his unexpected embrace, but his intolerance made her mind blaze with rage.

"Stay away from my brother. I mean it," Hugo ordered as he turned on his heel.

He marched out of the kitchen and made his way to the front door without hesitation. As she followed, Melissa doubted whether Hugo had spent time with her father after all.

4 CHAPTER

Melissa spent the whole night staring at the ceiling with wide eyes and a racing heart. She tangled her sweaty body in the sheets to remove Hugo's scent from her skin, but it only made her think about him more until she finally drifted off.

The next morning, Melissa watched the sunrise in peace as she sipped a steaming cup of Earl Grey. Images of the previous night flickered through her mind as she prepared for the day ahead when her ringtone distracted her.

Melissa glanced at the screen to see her mother calling and she gave a heavy sigh. She pulled her jumper over her head and answered the call.

"Good morning, Mum, you're up early."

"Good morning, Mandy, a day like this should not be wasted. We have a lot to do today."

Melissa rolled her eyes. "Mum, you're exaggerating. How long can hair and make-up possibly take?"

"It can take anywhere from an hour to several hours depending on the equipment and base I have to work on. When should I expect you to pick me up?"

"I was just about to leave. Shall we say in 20 minutes?"

"Perfect, I'm ready."

Melissa ended the call and hurried to the car. Her mind was still puzzled over Hugo's unexpected visit and her reaction to it.

She couldn't deny the odd chemistry between them that made her knees weak and her heart race at the same time. His presence was intimidating and imposed respect, which only made her want to do exactly the opposite. Whereas with Andres, she had found their encounter at the funeral very natural and easy.

Her mother was waiting in the driveway of her house and hopped into Melissa's rental as soon as she slowed the car. She eyed Melissa's cosy jumper and leggings with disgust.

"I see you have little thought of other people's opinions," her mother said, sniffing with disapproval. "What if Andres showed up at your house uninvited?"

Touché

Her mother's innocent words brought Melissa back to Hugo's unexpected appearance and hungry eyes, but she forced herself to remain present.

"Well, if he doesn't appreciate me for who I am, we can't be such a good match after all."

Melissa's mother rolled her eyes. "Mandy, why do you have to be so *complicated*? It's common courtesy to at least run a brush through your hair before leaving the house!"

Melissa quickly eyed her mother and grinned. The nickname her mother used didn't really match her full name. She had preferred the one her father had given her, but now with her father being gone, she was happy to have shared it only with him.

Melissa observed the traffic and forced a cheery smile.

"Then it must be your lucky day as my hair has never looked better," she replied, shaking her head to allow her golden locks to bounce on her shoulders.

During the twenty-four hours she had been in the small town, the seaside had already given her hair an added shine and much-needed volume, which she tried to compensate for with expensive hair care products in London.

Naturally, the authentic sea breeze was always better than a bottle, she thought and briefly brushed her hair back.

"That's not the point!" her mother snapped, crossing her hands over her chest.

Melissa turned into the familiar street and parked on the side of her father's driveway. She helped her mother out of the car and followed her inside.

"Oh, *sweetheart*, it's so warm and cosy here!" her mother exclaimed. "How did you manage to settle in so fast?"

Melissa dropped her keys onto the kitchen table and her thoughts returned to Hugo.

She huffed at his demand to cancel her date with Andres and wished she had argued back more, but his overwhelming presence and seducing cologne had clouded her thoughts. Had she sounded desperate?

"Melissa, are you listening to me?"

Her mother's voice brought her back to reality and she blinked. "Sorry, Mum, I missed your last words, what?"

Her mother sniffed at her. "I just said the house looks liveable again. It's such a shame no one lives here full time."

Her mother gazed around the kitchen with a curious smile, and Melissa worried that she'd be expected to stay.

She cleared her throat and sat down at the table, hanging her jacket over the back of the chair. "Don't get any ideas, will you? Like I said many times, I'm just visiting for the weekend."

"Yes, yes…I know," her mother said with a dismissive tone. "Come on, we've no time to waste. We need to get you ready for tonight."

Before Melissa could prepare a pot of tea, her mother strode toward the stairs and headed upstairs. Melissa sighed and followed her. She sat quietly on her bed and watched her mother go through her small weekender and then her old closet.

"I can't believe you didn't bring *anything* remotely presentable for the weekend!" her mother exclaimed as she rifled through Melissa's holiday bag.

Melissa rolled her eyes. "Mum, I came here to attend Patrick's funeral, not to go on dates and entertain myself."

Her mother brushed her forehead. "I know, Mandy, but regardless, you should always be ready for opportunities like this and prepare yourself a little bit, don't you think?"

"Well, I do have my little black dress and pumps from yesterday," Melissa suggested.

Melissa's mother gaped with horror. "Don't be absurd! You can't wear your *funeral* dress on a *date!* Especially as you *met* your date at the same funeral! What is *wrong* with you, Melissa?"

Melissa sniggered with amusement. "Good point, Mum. I guess I'm so used to it by now. I wear black dresses all the time at the office, at parties and at after-work drinks, it's practical and always looks elegant. "

Her mother nodded with satisfaction. "Well, that's why you have me to guide you, Mandy. Lucky you."

"Lucky me, indeed," Melissa repeated with sarcasm, rolling her eyes.

Her mother smiled, oblivious to Melissa's tone, and unzipped a large make-up bag on the desk.

"Mum, don't you think this is a slight overkill? You know I prefer to keep it simple," Melissa said, eyeing all the tubes and palettes as she took a seat.

Her mother grinned. "I wanted to come prepared as I didn't know what you had brought with you, and based on what I have seen so far, you're lucky that I did. "

"I didn't know I needed all this stuff on my face for a simple make-up look."

"You don't as you have very good foundation on your face, this only gives us a little bit of choice as we don't know yet what you're going to wear."

Melissa widened her eyes, surprised by the genuine compliment, which was not typical for her mother who was a master of complaining.

Her mother placed a few rollers in her hair and applied a brown base of brown eyeshadow to her eyelids, adding a plum hue to bring out Melissa's blue eyes. She made her pupils pop with a few coats of jet-black mascara and the plum shade of lipstick complemented her peachy foundation and blush.

A few minutes later, her mother removed the rollers and stepped back to eye her daughter.

"Voila, Mandy, I have to say, you look stunning! Even I would want to date you!" her mother chirped, closing the last eye shadow palette.

Melissa grinned. "Mum, please never say that again. I think that's considered child abuse."

Her mother chuckled and said, "Well, you look gorgeous, and this look is so easy to achieve, even for work."

Melissa raised her eyebrows. It was the first time she had heard her mother even remotely support her choice to move out of the small town and build a career.

"Anyway, what do you think?" her mother asked.

Melissa touched her hair and admired her new look in the mirror. "I look so different."

"Well, good different?" her mother pressed.

Melissa nodded. "I think so. I mean, it looks *amazing*, just not exactly like me."

"I know, *sweetheart*, and to be honest, I didn't even realise the results before I finished," her mother said, stroking Melissa's hair softly. "I *must* be very talented."

"Of course, Mum, what else could it be?" Melissa said with a sarcastic tone.

This time, Melissa's mother noticed her tone and said, "Obviously I had a good base to start with."

Melissa grinned through the mirror. "Thank you, Mum."

"Well, if you *really* think about it, even the base is something *I* created, once upon a time."

Melissa put down the hand mirror and stared at her mother. "Mum, why is it that you have to ruin every simple compliment with a side note?"

"Well *sweetheart*, who would argue with the truth?"

Melissa rolled her eyes. "Never mind – which dress should I wear?"

Her mother darted over to the closet and pulled out an icy blue gown with long sleeves and a sensual cut.

"Wait, this isn't my dress," Melissa said, touching the light fabric.

"I know, Mandy, luckily I threw a couple of outfits together just in case!" her mother replied with triumph.

Melissa glared at her mother and gazed at the dress in her hands.

"I'm not joking, where did you get this dress?"

"Oh, *sweetheart*, it's something I bought some time ago but never had a chance to wear," her mother explained. "I think it would look great on you with your make-up and all."

Melissa eyed the elegant garment as doubt overwhelmed her. She had to admit, it was a beautiful, elegant dress with a sensual cut. It wasn't too revealing, on the contrary, it left much for the imagination, which was refreshing considering the mini dresses she had witnessed in London on Friday nights on her way home from the office.

"I don't know, Mum. It's a beautiful dress, but I'm not sure it's my style," Melissa hesitated. "I never really wear colours apart from black and occasionally beige."

Melissa's mother stared at her with pity. "I know, *sweetheart*, but that's why you should give it a try. Who knows, you might be pleasantly surprised."

Melissa opened her mouth to respond when her mother's phone chimed. She raised her finger to silence her with a smile and answered the phone. Melissa turned her eyes back to the mirror and touched her bouncy new locks whilst listening to her mother's childish giggle over the phone.

"Oh stop, *darling*, of course I have time for you," her mother said, brushing the air and grinning flirtatiously as if the person was standing in front of her. "No, I'm not doing anything special at the moment. Sure, let's meet there in the next half an hour or so?"

Melissa rolled her eyes at the sudden turn of events. Her mother always got bored with her daughter only to find interest in something more glamorous. She watched her mother carefully collect the makeup equipment from the table and close her bag.

"Right, Mandy, as much fun as this has been, I'm afraid there is another engagement that requires my presence shortly. I hope you don't mind."

Without waiting for Melissa's reply, she turned on her heels and walked toward the staircase. Melissa grinned to her back and lifted the small suitcase her mother had left for her to carry down. She followed her to the front door.

"Have fun tonight, *sweetheart,* and enjoy!" her mother said, kissing Melissa on both cheeks and grabbing her bag from Melissa.

"I'll do my very best and thank you for all your help," Melissa said, putting a brave smile on her face.

Her mother nodded and turned away when Melissa spoke quickly. "Do you want me to drive you to your next engagement?"

Regardless of their difficult relationship, she instantly regretted not showing more appreciation for the hard work her mother had done. After all, she was her only living parent now.

"Oh no, don't be silly," her mother protested. "I'll find my own way. Besides, you need to finish getting ready!"

Melissa nodded. "OK, I'll talk to you tomorrow on my way back?"

"You better; I want all the details of tonight!" her mother replied. "Speak soon, Mandy."

Melissa smiled as she closed the door and rested her head against the cold wood. Her head throbbed behind her eyes, and she considered again calling off the evening with Andres, but she didn't want all her mother's effort to go to waste. Plus, she could use a nice evening out.

Melissa returned to her old bedroom and eyed the dress her mother had picked up for her. It was a beautiful dress and just as her mother had said, it would emphasise her figure and looks perfect, so after a short while of consideration, she slid into the dress.

She turned to look in the mirror and her eyes bulged with surprise. The fabric was soft but firm and the dress hugged her curvy figure like a glove and brought more attention to her peachy behind. Its mid-length emphasized her narrow ankles and made her legs look longer than they were. Melissa smiled at her newfound beauty and twirled in front of the mirror.

Suddenly, Hugo's face appeared in her mind as she imagined flaunting her defined figure in front of him.

Over my dead body, she thought and shook the thought away. Now was definitely not the time to sacrifice any thought to Andres's arrogant older brother. She gave a stern look at the clock in the room.

It was time to go.

Melissa reapplied her lipstick in the mirror and threw a black blazer over her arms. She slipped into her black high heels and hurried out to her car. She had decided to drive after all as she didn't want to be dependent on anyone, even though she was sure Andres would be a perfect gentleman and send someone to take her home if she asked.

She drove silently through the tortuous road towards the Ferrero mansion to the most affluent yet private part of the town.

She hadn't been near the mansion since the time ten years ago when she had followed the beachline for hours and eventually ended up at the entrance of one of their private beaches. Contrary to her normal behaviour, she had broken through the small fence and sat down on the clean, white sand to enjoy the silence until she heard quick steps behind her.

"What are you doing here, this is private property!"

Melissa stood up and quickly turned around like a rabbit caught in the spotlight.

"Cat got your tongue?" the boy had asked with a soft foreign accent, which Melissa now recognised as Hugo's.

She had been so caught off guard that she had quickly run away without saying a word, leaving Hugo to watch her go.

That day had been just after the late Mrs Ferrero had drowned, and since then, she hadn't dared to enter the private land of the Ferrero family, before Andres's invitation.

After a short drive, Melissa cruised through the open gates and slowly drove along the well-kept driveway towards the Victorian castle. She gazed up at the stone walls of the two towers and admired the heavy door covered in Devil's Ivy. The fortress reminded her of the one in the fairy tales she used to read as a child.

Melissa stepped out of her car and enjoyed the beautiful scent of the blooming flower beds that stretched to the main gate as she strode towards the main entrance.

She knocked on the door and Andres opened it immediately.

"Good evening, Melissa, I'm glad you could make it," he greeted, pausing to look at his wrist. "On time."

Melissa smiled. "I'm glad you invited me, the place looks amazing and the fresh flower beds outside look divine."

"I'm glad you like them, Melissa," Andres replied. "May I take your blazer?"

"Oh, yes...thank you," Melissa hesitated, a little conscious of her new style, but she removed her blazer and handed it to her date.

Andres placed it on his lap and continued.

"I know your father was quite the green thumb, so I figured you would appreciate the effort."

Melissa blushed. "You did it to impress me?"

Andres chuckled. "Well, you can't blame me for trying, but I must disappoint you. The installation of the flower beds started last month after my accident. My father figured it would cheer me up since I will be spending more time here. Permanently."

"Oh, I didn't know you would be relocating here permanently," Melissa said, surprised.

"The house has been empty for such a long time."

Andres nodded and grinned. "I know, it's about time someone lived in it, don't you think? Anyway, let me give you a quick tour."

Andres turned in his wheelchair and gestured for Melissa to follow him. Melissa stepped inside the castle and closed the heavy door behind her.

"The engineers have finished installing the lift and ramps around the house for me so I can maintain my independence."

"Oh, that's impressive," Melissa said as she followed Andres into the glass lift. She waited for the lift to move before she opened her mouth again. "Is your father paying for the house's refurbishment?"

Melissa knew she was crossing the line, but she couldn't help being curious about the family they had all been second guessing for her entire life, but to her surprise, Andres didn't seem to mind her curiosity.

"God no, my father doesn't have anything to do with the finances of the house," Andres clarified. "My irresponsible brother is covering the costs, but it's the *least* he can do."

The lift halted and Andres beckoned for Melissa to step out first.

"Do you know the story of what happened?" Andres asked as he followed her.

Melissa shook her head.

"I can give you a quick summary rather than bore you with details." He smiled and continued. "Well, Patrick and I were partying in London with some friends, but we got too drunk to drive home. I knew Hugo was in town, passing through from one of his escapades with yet *another* woman…" Andres glanced at Melissa knowingly and continued. "As you might remember, my brother is never satisfied with one – so I asked if he could give us a lift."

Melissa tried to recall anything remotely of Hugo from their early years in the town, but for some reason, she really didn't have any recollection of him, let alone his love affairs. On the contrary, he had been extremely introverted for as long as Melissa could remember, but there was absolutely no reason for his brother to lie for him.

"Anyhow, Hugo turned out to be drunk, but we stupidly got into his car anyway. During the journey, Hugo crashed into a lorry in the other lane. Patrick died instantly, but for me – permanent spinal cord injury…hence the chair."

"Oh…"

Melissa gulped at Andres's tragic story but his blasé comment about Hugo circled in her mind.

*Never satisfied with one woman…*she thought as last night's events flashed through her mind.

Now it made sense. Her heart deflated at Hugo dismissing her as one of his many conquests.

"Are you ok, Melissa? You've gone very pale all of sudden, do you want to sit down? I know the lift can make people lightheaded if you're not used to it."

Melissa shook her head. "Oh no, I'm fine. I didn't have a proper lunch today, so I guess I'm hungry."

Andres nodded. "Say no more, let's go back down to enjoy dinner and we can resume the tour later."

Andres turned towards the lift again and the two of them remained silent all the way down.

Once they reached the bottom, Melissa gasped as they entered the towering dining area that had a lengthy table with twelve seats and a crystal chandelier hanging from the ceiling. Multiple white candles adorned the table, and the firelight made the chandelier's crystal droplets glisten around the room. Despite the glamour, Andres' family had made the effort to move the furniture around and add disability rails for Andres to move through the room with ease.

"It's stunning in here!" Melissa exclaimed.

Andres beamed. "I know, it's pretty breathtaking. It's actually a signature design of my mother's before she passed away. She always loved the romantic style. In fact, my mother did all the internal alternations in the house, but she was always adamant to leave the exterior in its original state. She considered it too romantic to destroy, and of course, my father couldn't argue with her…he was too in love."

Melissa smiled softly and gazed around the room like an excited child as she followed Andres to the end of the table.

The twelfth chair had been removed for Andres, but the one next to his spot had been reserved for Melissa.

"I would pull the chair for you, but you know how it is," Andres said with a sigh.

"Oh, don't worry about it," Melissa brushed off as she took a seat, glancing around the massive room that could have catered for tens of people, yet they were dining alone.

"I think the chef has prepared lobster with garlic and vegetables tonight, but I'll make sure we have mint tea afterwards, so we don't have any breath issues," Andres said.

Melissa laughed. "Good idea! But only if we both have it, so we won't then smell it on each other."

Andres beamed. "Deal then! I hope you like lobster?"

Melissa smiled and placed a napkin on her lap. "Yes, I'm a pescatarian, so I only eat seafood."

Andres popped open a bottle of white wine and raised his eyebrows.

"Wow, lucky I didn't offer you veal!" he said with amusement as the chef brought out the appetisers.

"Well, I would have felt extremely guilty as it would have been my job to inform you of any allergies or food restrictions before our date," Melissa said and smiled.

"Indeed." Andres nodded, pleased with her reply.

They ate in silence, and after finishing their appetisers, they discussed Andres's career in London, his university experience, and the accident. They briefly talked about Melissa's career as well, and Andres questioned whether she would ever move back to Canford Cliffs. The conversation reverted to Andres' accident a few times and he couldn't help but badmouth his twin brother.

"Andres, you've mentioned your brother quite a lot now during the dinner," she said, wiping the corners of her mouth with a napkin. "Is Hugo staying here with you to help out?"

Andres narrowed his eyes. "Well, he arrived yesterday, but I haven't seen him since. He tends to stay in his part of the house or the local pub drinking his brains out. Why, have you seen him?"

Her passionate kiss with Hugo filled her mind, but she shook her head and avoided Andres' gaze. "Of course not, I just wondered since you've mentioned him quite a few times tonight."

"Well, I'm sure you would as well if he'd ruined your life!" Andres snapped. "Unlike him, I can't *practically* find a woman because of the state *he* put me in!"

Melissa's eyes bulged with surprise, and she fell silent. Andres sighed and a sweet smile returned to his face.

"I'm sorry for my outburst, Melissa, I didn't mean to direct my frustration towards you," Andres apologised, and he buried his face into his hands in such a manner that Melissa felt sorry for him.

"It's okay, I understand," Melissa said.

"It's ironic, isn't it?" Andres exclaimed, sobbing. "I waited so long to build my career and create my own path without thinking about women, but I'm now unable to attract a woman's desire because of this stupid wheelchair!"

Melissa's heart broke for Andres. She stroked his back and turned to face him.

"Andres, I'm sure there are millions of women who would die to be your wife and share their life with you," Melissa assured, touching his hand over the table. "You're attractive, charming, *and* you have a good sense of humour. Traits any woman would be stupid to overlook."

Andres eyed her with suspicion. "Are you saying you wouldn't mind this wheelchair at all?"

Melissa withdrew her hand and weighed her response.

"If I loved someone, absolutely not. Your wheelchair would have nothing to do with how I felt about you."

Andres nodded and leaned closer to her. "What about the sexual interaction... and children – I assume you want one?"

Melissa straightened her back and blushed with embarrassment. She didn't want to share such detail with a person she hardly knew, but for the sake of good manners, she forced a smile and continued.

"Well, I'm sure there would be a way to enjoy a physical relationship, and there are many options for people who want children, so I wouldn't worry about it too much."

Andres grinned. "God, Melissa, you are a person with such a good heart. I feel more alive than ever since my accident."

"I'm glad, you should be happy to be alive. Life itself is a miracle."

"Say no more," Andres replied, and he lifted his wine glass. "To us, Melissa, and a bright future."

Melissa laughed with warmth and raised her glass in the air. "I'll drink to that."

The light conversation continued for the rest of the dinner and Melissa stood from the table to excuse herself.

"Sorry, where's the bathroom?" she asked.

"From the main hall to the right and up, you can't miss it," Andres directed.

Melissa thanked him and headed towards the spiral staircase and realised how much the wine had affected her. Her vision blurred and she had to grab the handle to get upstairs.

Once she reached the top and staggered towards the first door, a familiar, musky scent caught her attention. Melissa touched the door handle when she noticed the shadow of a dark figure reflected on a framed painting on the wall. She gasped and turned, staring into the corridor. She couldn't see anything suspicious, but she could sense someone watching her.

"Melissa, is everything ok up there? Did you find the bathroom?" Andres called from downstairs.

"Yeah, I found it; everything's fine!" Melissa yelled back.

She used the bathroom as fast as possible and returned to Andres, who had moved to the main salon. He waited in front of a massive fireplace and beckoned her towards two more glasses of wine on the mantelpiece. Another open bottle sat in a metal bucket of ice.

"I don't think I should drink much more, I don't want to disrespect you by drinking and driving," Melissa declined, eyeing the full glass.

"Nonsense, Melissa," Andres dismissed, and he wheeled closer to the table and took a long sip of the cold wine. "Come and sit with me on the sofa."

Andres used his arm strength to lift himself onto the couch and Melissa sat beside him with her wine glass.

"Your athletic background seems to have come in handy with the wheelchair," Melissa observed.

Andres nodded briefly. "Yep, even if the legs don't work, my hands are stronger than ever."

Andres winked and made a sexual gesture with his fingers. Melissa raised her eyebrow at the vulgar expression but forced a fake giggle. She didn't want to upset him now he could finally focus on something positive.

Andres sipped his drink and placed his empty glass on the table before them, and Melissa did the same. "To be honest, Melissa, sharing a meal and catching up is not the only reason why I invited you here today."

"Oh, is that so?"

Andres twisted his fingers and bit his lip. "I must confess that I have always been fond of you. Some would even call it love, but I never approached you when we were younger." He smiled apologetically. "None of us thought you were very approachable."

Melissa gaped at Andres' revelation. "Oh dear, Andres, I had no idea!"

"Well, you do now," Andres replied with a grin. He wrapped his arm around her shoulders and pulled her into his chest. "I know you're not dating anyone at the moment, and I understand that you are focused on your career and all, but wouldn't it be nice to share the burden of building your career with someone who has a mutual interest in life?"

Melissa remained silent and thought back to Hugo. "Who knows, perhaps I could introduce you to some of the businesspeople I know in London," Andres added. "I could help you skyrocket your firm's portfolio!"

"I don't know, Andres, I'm not sure it's a good enough reason to start dating," Melissa doubted.

Andres' mouth quivered into a wolf smile. "Oh, I must have explained myself poorly, Melissa. I don't want to *just* date you, I want you to marry me."

"What?!" Melissa exclaimed, incredulous.

"Of course, I wouldn't dare to offer you anything short-term. You are way more valuable than that," Andres clarified.

The mysterious meaning of his words was left unnoticed as she eyed him in shock.

"But you don't even know me!" Melissa cried.

"Sometimes, you don't have to spend years getting to know someone before you realise that they're the one. Don't you believe in that, Melissa?"

Melissa fell silent again as she considered the lack of experience she had had with love and relationships. Could it be that easy? She had no idea.

"Melissa, I mean it, all I want to do is make you happy. Who knows, maybe you will fall in love with me eventually?" Andres pressed, tugging her face closer to his.

Andres' alcohol-filled breath tickled her face as she allowed him to lean in and kiss her, but the sudden sound of glass shattering outside the room cut the moment. Melissa jumped back and covered her mouth.

"Don't worry, it's probably one of the waiters," Andres assured.

Embarrassed that she had let both brothers kiss her within the same twenty-four hours, Melissa got to her feet and rushed for the exit. "I need to go."

"Wait, Melissa!" Andres yelled, but Melissa didn't stop until she heard a loud bump behind her.

She turned to see Andres on the floor a short distance from his wheelchair. Out of guilt, Melissa assisted him back into his chair.

"Thank you, Melissa," Andres said with a smile. "You see, I *do* need you."

Melissa returned his smile but remained silent. The last twenty-four hours had filled her with too much confusion to handle, so she wanted to get home to clear her head.

"Please marry me, Melissa! You would make me a very happy man!" Andres begged.

Melissa sighed. "I don't know, Andres, I barely know you and it's not the best way to start a marriage. I always thought it should start with a great love story."

A dark shadow appeared on Andres' beautiful face and his voice sharpened. "Really? Let me remind you that a great love story didn't save your parents' marriage."

Melissa frowned. "How do you know that?"

"Please, everyone in town knew about it. Your mother couldn't stop talking about it until *my mother* told her to keep her marital problems within the family and work them out with your father," Andres explained as he wheeled closer like a preying tiger.

Melissa blushed at her mother's familiar behaviour. She had always been a gossip, but Melissa had secretly hoped that she didn't blab her marital problems with everyone in the town. She had clearly been wrong.

Andres softened his voice and stopped in front of her. "Think about it, Melissa. At least we could avoid all those problems by being a team."

"I will think about it," Melissa whispered, eyeing her shoes.

She turned to leave when Andres said something that halted her in her tracks.

"I didn't want to be the one to tell you, but if we married, I would be able to assist you with the outstanding debt held against your father's house. I'm sure you don't want to lose it."

Melissa jerked her head up. "What are you talking about?"

Andres smiled apologetically. "It seems that your mother is more high maintenance as an ex-wife than your father thought, and she incurred a large debt over the years after their divorce. Your father had eventually settled some outstanding bills against the house's value, but he didn't have the time to finish the repayments, so the house now belongs to the bank unless you have the cash to pay it."

The blood drained from Melissa's face, and she turned pale. "My father wouldn't do that! Not without telling me first."

"I think you'll find he would, Melissa," Andres said. "Why would an old man admit his love for a woman who only cared about his monthly financial support?"

"Oh my God!" Melissa cried, recognising Andres' description of her father, who always spoke lovingly about her mother despite all the demands she had put on him over the years.

"I know, it's tragic, and I'm sorry to be the bearer of the bad news," Andres said, lifting his hand to caress her cheek.

Melissa brushed his hand away and stepped back from Andres' touch. "I have to go."

Andres opened his arms in surrender. "Think about it and check the facts if you like, but it's common knowledge. I'm surprised you know nothing about it."

"I will, thanks," she said.

Melissa dashed towards the door as multiple questions filled her mind. None of what Andres said made sense to her.

"Leave the car behind, will you? I'll call you an uber," Andres called after her again and pulled his mobile phone from his pocket. "I would hate for you to disrespect me by drinking and driving."

His ironic remark was left unnoticed as the uncomfortable silence stood between them. Melissa tapped her heel on the floor and brushed her neck nervously. She didn't want to come across as ungrateful, but she couldn't wait to get home to prove Andres wrong, though, deep inside, she was sure there was a hint of truth in Andres's words. She just hoped that the damage done was fixable.

"Ok, the uber should be here any minute now. You're free to wait at the main gate if you wish, it shouldn't take more than a couple of minutes," Andres said and closed his phone.

Melissa nodded and closed the door behind her. She hurried to the main entrance and shivered as she waited a few minutes for her driver.

When the Uber arrived, she hopped inside and suddenly remembered that she had left her only blazer behind.

"Shit!" she exclaimed under her breath, already dreading her return to get it before she returned to London.

Melissa exhaled and tried to erase both brothers and her family's debt from her thoughts. She let the heat of the car warm her skin and drift her to sleep.

***

Hugo winced as he picked small shards of glass from his palm. He never planned to eavesdrop on his brother's date, but listening to Andres' proposal stabbed him deep for a reason he couldn't explain. He hadn't thought about Melissa for a long time before Patrick's funeral and his visit to her father's house, but now she entered his mind more than he liked to admit.

His childhood obsession had merely been down to the curiosity of a teenage boy and an escape from the sibling rivalry his brother had taken to the extreme over his unreasonable jealousy concerning their mother.

Still, Melissa's stubborn character mixed with the innocent way she flaunted herself in front of him made her irresistible to him. Hugo still had no intention of pursuing his ridiculous childhood crush, but his brother's proposal and her obvious consideration made him squeeze the glass in his hand, the edges penetrating his skin as the calmness he craved engulfed him.

5 CHAPTER

On Monday morning, Melissa woke up early and made her way to the local bank to verify the story Andres had told her. She didn't doubt him as his description of her parents fit, but she wondered whether Andres had exaggerated the circumstances to get her to marry him.

She ripped off a queue number and sat in the waiting area. She opened a sandwich she had bought from a local supermarket, as she had been too nervous to eat anything at home, but before she could take the first bite...

"Number 15, please," the young receptionist yelled.

Melissa stood from her seat and approached the desk. She handed all her father's paperwork to the male assistant and gulped with nerves.

"I need to know the outstanding debt of my father's accounts; invoices, credit cards, direct debits, anything you can find," Melissa requested, taking a seat.

After a few clicks on the computer, the assistant informed her that her father had been paying her mother's credit card bills until he passed away, and he had also settled her housing costs since she had moved to her rental property after their divorce. Melissa also discovered that her father had successfully managed to cover the cost of two independent households until he stopped working full-time two years ago due to early signs of heart problems, which Melissa had known nothing about. Out of desperation, he had obviously set some of the repayments against the value of the house, as Andres had explained, which he had never been able to recover again, *but had been too proud to involve anyone,* Melissa thought.

She swallowed her disgust with her mother and forced back the emerging tears.

"Why didn't anyone inform me when my father died? I'm sure the solicitor knew all about it when looking into the existing assets?" Melissa questioned.

"I'm afraid I don't have an answer to that, Madam. The direct debits have gone from his current account until the system informed us of the insufficient funds, which is when we started sending invoices. All of which have been left without action."

Melissa frowned.

The mailbox at her father's house had been empty, which meant that someone must have picked them up after he had died without informing her or anyone else.

Her mother's face flashed through her mind, but she gritted her teeth and forced herself to remain calm and polite.

"So, have you been contacted by my father's solicitor at all?"

The question made perfect sense to anyone else, but knowing her father, Melissa dreaded the reply; she was almost sure he hadn't appointed a solicitor before he had died.

The customer service assistant shook his head. "I'm afraid not."

Melissa let a long breath out and nodded. "How much is the outstanding debt in total?"

The customer service assistant turned to the monitor. "If you want to keep the bank from repossessing the house, the monthly repayments would be £2,300 per month."

Melissa gasped. "What the hell did my mother buy with her credit cards?"

The assistant smiled with apology in his eyes. "Well, it's actually quite reasonable if you think that he managed to cover two household costs plus additional expenses from one part-time income and credit cards."

"Still, it doesn't make any sense!" Melissa cried, rubbing her temples. "Can I split the repayments over several years? If I pick up a second job in the city, I could potentially pay £700 per month."

The assistant turned back to the monitor and continued to type into the system, but he let the air out between his teeth. "I'm afraid not. The banks don't like to own anything they repossess, so they prefer to sell the assets below the market price as quickly as possible to avoid any further risks."

"Can't you just wait and make a new deal with me?" Melissa pressed. "This is the bank where my father had all his money and business for decades, I think the bank *owes* him that."

The gentleman took off his reading glasses and folded them in front of her. "With all due respect, *Madam*, this bank is not a property investment company, and the market is very unstable at the moment. This bank has taken care of local businesses for over a century and has been stable through thick and thin, which wouldn't have been possible without strict business policies, but your request to withhold your father's property for lower monthly repayments goes against that."

"I see," Melissa said, defeated.

She felt all the strength slowly disappear from her body.

"I'm sorry, *Madam*, I wish there was something I could do," the assistant said.

Melissa sighed. "What about the rental market here? There must be tourists visiting during the summer. I could rent the house out and cover the repayments with rental income."

The gentleman nodded. "From the bank's point of view, we don't really care as long as the repayments are paid on time in legal ways, but from what we have seen in recent years, the rental market consists of flats mainly. Plus, it's slowed down considerably as many young people now relocate to bigger cities for studies and work. Regarding houses specifically, people prefer to buy, and based on previous experiences, many short-term rentals have resulted in unnecessary damages caused by careless tenants, which is fine if you're ready for those kinds of battles."

Melissa listened as the assistant filled her idea with holes. She thought she'd be able to repay the money in no time, but she couldn't bear to lose all her father's hard work.

The assistant considered her silence and eagerly handed her a card.

"I can give you the contact details for the local property agency if you wish. The value of the houses close to the beach has increased over the years, so you might be able to make a good deal."

Melissa smiled. "That's fine, Sir, you have been ever so helpful today, I think I will see myself out now."

Melissa stood and shouldered her bag.

"Don't worry, Madam, you still have time to decide what to do," he reassured. "These things tend to take time."

Melissa turned around and a glimpse of hope filled her eyes. "How much time?"

The assistant shrugged and said, "Couple of months, top."

On the way home, Melissa parked on her mother's street and considered forcing her mother to find a job and share the repayments, but even if she agreed, which was highly unlikely as her mother had been a housewife all her life, they wouldn't make enough between them to pay the bank.

Andres's proposal popped into her mind, but Melissa quickly brushed it off in an instant. She could never allow herself to do such a thing for money.

But what about for your father? a small voice asked in her head.

If Melissa let the bank sell her childhood home in a low-market auction, the potential buyer may not be a family who planned to buy the house to create memories.

They could be an investor who wanted to tear down the house and build something much bigger, Melissa thought.

She wasn't oblivious to the value of the ground the house sat upon, especially as it was just a stone's throw away from the best beach in town.

Melissa sighed tiredly.

Despite living in London, she knew she couldn't bear to sell the only place where she had shared all her memories with her father.

There must be another way, she thought as she started the engine and turned the car around.

After a twenty-minute drive, she arrived at the Ferrero mansion again.

***

"Melissa, what a pleasant surprise!" Andres exclaimed as he opened the door.

"Hi, Andres, I'm so sorry to show up uninvited, but I wanted to speak to you before I left."

Andres nodded and wheeled aside to let Melissa enter the house. "Melissa, please, you don't need an invitation to stop by, I'm actually glad you did. I worried that our conversation yesterday made you never want to speak to me again."

Melissa laughed and stepped inside. "Don't worry, Andres, if I was nervous, it was simply because I've just never been proposed to before. I guess any woman would have reacted the same."

Andres smiled and closed the door behind her. "I guess you are right, poor timing. Would you like to sit down to discuss this over a coffee?"

"That would be great," Melissa replied, shivering in her cardigan.

Despite the endless sun during the summertime, the days in September had brought a never-ending chill to the town.

Melissa followed Andres to the main living room where the wood logs from yesterday continued to burn in the fireplace. She darted towards the flames and held her hands over the fire.

Andres entered the room behind her.

"You left so abruptly yesterday that you forgot your blazer," Andres said, grabbing it from a hanger. "I hope you don't mind, but I had it dry cleaned and ironed. I know many people in London are very particular over who dry cleans their laundry, but I can assure you that Mrs Whittle is pure gold when it comes to housekeeping, she knows everything."

Melissa smiled and walked over to him to take the blazer. "Andres, you shouldn't have, but I'm ever so grateful for your effort."

"The pleasure was all mine," he said and signaled to the butler to bring in some afternoon coffee.

The young boy disappeared immediately to comply with his request.

Andres wheeled closer to the table. It didn't take long before the butler brought two mugs of steaming coffee into the room and a small tray of sweet and savoury bites.

"Thank you," Andres said, and the butler left the room. "Help yourself to the snacks on the table as well, they're all homemade."

Melissa made herself comfortable in the armchair and Andres pulled himself onto the sofa, just as he had done the day before. She glanced at Andres' boyish expression, and for a split second, he looked even more like Hugo. Melissa waited for the butterflies to fill her stomach, but nothing.

Melissa brought the cup to her lips and grabbed a sweet treat from the table.

"You were right about my father's financial situation," she said.

A muscle moved on Andres' face. "I'm sorry to hear. I thought someone had already told you."

"I wish they had," Melissa said with a sigh. "At least then I could have helped sooner and we wouldn't be in this situation."

"Well, you need to consider yourself lucky on some level."

Melissa jerked her head up and frowned. "Which part of this makes me *lucky?*"

Andres slurped his coffee and met Melissa's defensive stare. "You still have options before you lose the house - start paying the repayments or reconsider my offer."

Melissa paused and weighted her response. "You are right but paying off a debt shouldn't be the reason to get married."

"Well, it isn't... certainly for me," Andres said, helping himself to a savoury treat. "As I said to you, I have been in love with you for the best part of my life and nothing could make me happier than having you by my side. Now, it's down to you to decide whether I'm a good enough reason for you to marry me."

Melissa blushed as his words clearly implied that she only considered marrying him to offset her father's debt, which wasn't far from the truth, but she forced her head high.

Melissa exhaled. "Before I say yes, I need to know the truth about your condition and what our life would be like."

Andres beamed and shuffled to the end of the sofa, closer to Melissa. "Of course, I didn't expect anything less from you. As I mentioned earlier, the physical part of the relationship will be tricky for me as I can't perform like other men, but I can promise that you would feel completely satisfied and fulfilled."

Melissa blushed and glared at her feet. "I'm not sure I understand, shouldn't we get to know each other a little bit before we make such a drastic conclusion? Who knows, I might even disappoint you."

Andres's mouth quivered into a wolf smile. "Melissa, you could never disappoint me! On the contrary, I have waited for this moment for a long time."

Andres hopped back into his wheelchair and whizzed over to Melissa. He caressed the side of her face and smiled. "Do you find me attractive?"

Melissa studied Andres' beautiful face and chiselled features. Although his presence didn't give her butterflies, Andres had always been handsome, and the close resemblance to his twin brother made Melissa pull her head down in a shy manner.

"Yes, I do find you attractive," Melissa replied, avoiding his gaze.

"There you go then, problem solved," Andres said, and he clapped his hands and helped himself to another savoury treat.

"Hold on, Andres, I didn't say yes."

"But your answers implied that you will."

Melissa stayed quiet, weighing her options.

"And what if it doesn't work?" Melissa questioned, her heart sinking even more by the second.

Andres dipped his brow. "What do you mean?"

"What if the marriage simply doesn't work out, what should we do?"

"Well, I would treat it like any other marriage and assume that you wouldn't flee at the first opportunity," Andres replied, filling Melissa with guilt. "Especially considering my disability."

Melissa twisted her hands in her lap and twiddled her fingers. "Of course, I wouldn't do that but–"

"It's settled then, that's all I'm asking from you," Andres interrupted. "Now, if you will excuse me, there are some errands I need to do."

Andres turned in his chair and headed for the exit, leaving Melissa uncomfortable but desperate. She felt rushed to make up her mind, but she also feared that Andres would change his mind and she would lose the only opportunity to save her family home.

"Let's do it!" Melissa called after him.

Andres turned with a start. "Are you serious?"

Melissa stood from the armchair, full of determination. "Yes, I'm serious, let's get married."

Andres beamed and wheeled back to Melissa. He pulled her into his lap and she forced her arms around his neck.

"You've just made me the happiest man on earth!" Andres exclaimed, and he leaned in to kiss her.

Melissa kissed him back, but unlike Hugo, Andres didn't create a passionate storm in her mind.

"I hope I'm making the right choice," Melissa whispered, reminding herself that marriage couldn't always be about the butterflies.

Plus, Andres had been nothing but a gentleman to her, and she still had her friends and career in London.

"I hope so too," Andres said. He snuggled into Melissa's hair and let his lip quiver into a malicious smile. "I hope so too."

6 CHAPTER

The next morning, Melissa woke up to her phone vibrating on her nightstand. She opened one eye and glared at the clock on the wall, only to realise that it was after 7 am. Swallowing her curse, she picked up her phone.

"Mmm, hello?"

"Mandy, sweetheart, are you still in bed?" her mother chirped on the other side of the phone.

She sighed and switched the phone to the other ear so she could lie back down in bed. "Yes, Mum, I wake up before 6 am every morning when I'm working so I thought it would be nice to sleep in for a change."

Her mother ignored her sarcastic response and continued the conversation casually. "Sure, so I just wanted to know how everything went yesterday. I hope you didn't completely embarrass yourself in front of Andres."

Suddenly, the flow of last night's events flooded into her mind and Melissa found herself completely awake. If only her mother knew.

"Well, it was nice. Good food and so on. You know how these things are."

"Really? So, nothing happened?"

Melissa grinned; she could see her mother's face falling from her lack of response to her gossip.

"Well, in that case, I don't wish to bother you longer, Mandy. I just wanted to know if you had a good time."

Melissa was about to thank her mother for the call when she suddenly realised that her mother would need to know what had happened and about the upcoming wedding. Hell, she was her only family left after all.

"Wait, Mum, actually… there is something I wanted to tell you. Do you have time for brunch today?"

"Well, I already had my breakfast, but I could do a quick coffee."

Melissa nodded even though she knew her mother couldn't see her. "Perfect, shall we say in the city centre at the small French coffee shop by the main street?"

"Sure, can you make it within an hour?"

If I don't apply any make-up, I'll have just enough time to shower and change, Melissa thought.

"Yep, see you in an hour," Melissa said and waited for her mother to cut the line.

How would she be able to break the news to her mother?

Melissa stepped into the small coffee shop and the bell rang to notify staff that someone had entered. One of the assistants welcomed her and showed her to the table.

Her mother had not arrived yet, which gave Melissa time to look around and admire the unique interior design. Each table and chair were different in build and colour, but they all seemed to fit very well together.

Would it work just as effortlessly in my marriage as well? Melissa thought.

It didn't take long for the sound of her mother's heels to echo through the coffee shop.

"Sorry for being late, I didn't plan to go out at this hour," her mother said, sitting down on the blue wooden chair.

"That's ok, Mum. I've only just arrived anyway," Melissa said and crossed her hands over the table to avoid picking her fingernails.

They quickly placed their orders with the waiter and talked about the weather whilst waiting for the coffees and croissants to arrive.

"So, you said you had something to tell me," her mother said, mixing sweetener into her steaming coffee.

"Well, yes, kind of…"

"So did you have a good time yesterday?" her mother prompted.

"Well, yes, kind of…"

Her mother huffed and dropped the tablespoon onto the table. "Mandy, please don't tell me you invited me for a coffee for this?"

"Ok ok, we had dinner and then Andres proposed to me!"

Her mother paused. "What do you mean he proposed? Like to go out again?"

"No, Mum. Marriage!"

For once, it looked like Melissa's news had left her mother speechless.

She frowned and said, "What do you mean marriage?"

"Like man and wife marriage?" Melissa replied as if it was obvious.

Her mother dropped her mug onto the table and turned her full attention to Melissa.

"Let me get this straight, Andres Ferrero said he wants to marry you?"

"Yes."

"Like happily ever after marriage?"

"Yes."

A short silence filled the air between them before her mother whispered, "And what did you say?"

Melissa weighed her response for a second.

"I said yes."

Her mother stoop up so quickly that the whole table moved, resulting in both of their coffees spilling over the white tablecloth.

"Mum, watch out!" Melissa cried, trying to save the little coffee there was left in the mugs.

"Oh Lord, this is the best news ever! Who would have thought that *my* daughter would be the next Mrs Ferrero!" She laughed out loud and grabbed the nearby waiter by his shoulders. "Did you know my daughter will marry Mr Andres Ferrero?"

"Mum, stop it, you're embarrassing us both!" Melissa said with amusement.

She quickly apologised to the waiter and send him away.

"Wait until everybody hears about this!" her mother said and fished out her mobile from her pocket.

"Is it really necessary?"

Her mother looked at her as if she had lost her mind. "It's not every day that my only daughter informs me that she is about to marry the only royalty in town. The Ferrero boys never bothered to come down from their shiny castle to visit anyone, but now this. This is news that needs to be shared!"

Suddenly, the image of Hugo flooded her mind, sipping his tea casually on the kitchen table, but she quickly shook the thought away and focused on her mother dialling *everyone* to spread the exciting news of the upcoming wedding.

7 CHAPTER

On the morning of the wedding, Melissa felt sick. Even though Andres had been nothing but a gentleman, she still wasn't sure if she was making the right choice.

They had decided to marry a month after Melissa's initial visit to Canford Cliffs, and it had been a joint decision to keep the ceremony plain and small. Although Andres had tried to convince Melissa to splurge on the wedding, Melissa had kept her mind and only purchased the necessities she thought she would need as a Mrs Andres Ferrero.

Her mother arrived at her father's house early and helped Melissa to slip into her mermaid-style wedding dress and a pair of nude high heels, which Melissa hoped would serve well at work or any other formal occasion she might attend as Andre's wife in the future. Melissa left her make-up choice to her mother, who used her creativity and focused on her skin and lips. She applied a heavy coat of black mascara to her long lashes, but instead of creating heavy shadows on her eyelids, she painted her lips with blood-red lipstick that made her blue irises pop.

"See, you don't always need heavy eye makeup when you can achieve the same outcome with a different style," her mother said and smoothed her curls when Melissa's alarm went off.

It was time.

When Melissa and her mother arrived at All Saints Church in Canford Cliffs, the area buzzed with local people wandering around the church to catch a peak of the famous son of Sir Daniel, who had tragically lost his mobility only months before the wedding.

Melissa looked at the crowd, took a deep breath and opened the car door. The chilly morning breeze gave her goosebumps as she held on tighter to the small bouquet of white lilies she had picked up for the day. She didn't even have to smile as her mother had left the car first and beamed brightly at everyone as if it was her shining moment.

Melissa couldn't help but smile at the absurdity of the situation before lowering her head and walking directly into the chapel.

She stopped for a moment to wait for her mother to enter and walk her up the aisle.

As soon as she reached Andres at the end of the aisle, the organ playing *Here Comes the Bride* stopped, and her mother took a seat in the front row.

Andres beamed at his fiancée and Melissa faked a smile in return.

Whilst listening to the vicar talking about the love and commitment to one another, Melissa couldn't help stealing a quick look of support from her mother.

"You may now kiss the bride…"

"Melissa?" Andres said and raised his eyebrow.

"Oh, what?"

She quickly returned to reality and looked at her soon-to-be husband.
If Andres had realised her sudden absence from the moment, he didn't seem to mind as he motioned for her to lean over for a kiss.

Suddenly, the wooden double doors crashed open and Melissa saw a dark figure slipping inside and taking a seat at the back of the chapel. The sudden beam of morning light blinded her for a moment as she squinted to see who had interrupted the ceremony so abruptly.

The hair on her back stood up on end and droplets of sweat formed on her upper lip as her eyes adjusted to the light.

Hugo.

She wasn't sure if she had silently mouthed his name as their eyes locked. His stare was dark and intense as if he tried to penetrate her soul. She tried to refocus her gaze on her newly-wedded husband, but she couldn't tear her eyes away from Hugo. Melissa instantly felt her body tense.

"Melissa, everyone is waiting…" Andres said, pulling her down. "The kiss?"

Melissa looked down at her husband and felt the heat building on her cheeks as she planted a platonic kiss on the corner of his lip.

It was beyond awkward, and Melissa only hoped that the redness on her cheeks wouldn't give her feelings away, but how could she now relax having her husband's twin brother at their wedding? A twin brother who had stolen a kiss from her not long ago.

"Would you like to say a few words?"

Melissa's eyes widened and she looked anxiously at Andres.

They had agreed on a short ceremony without vows as Melissa felt nervous speaking in public, but she also lacked the words for her new husband, whom she didn't know at all.

The silence echoed around the small chapel until Andres turned to speak to the crowd. "I know we agreed against sharing any vows publicly, but that's something we will do in the privacy of our home."

The crowd burst into laughter, but Andres raised his hand to continue.

"But I still would like to say that I'm forever grateful to Melissa for giving me this chance to love and cherish her just the way she deserves. It's not often that you can find a woman ready to fall for a broken man such as myself..."

He didn't have to finish as everyone stood up and clapped. Andres turned to her and said, "Now, I would like to give the floor to my lovely wife as I'm sure she would like to say something as well."

Melissa stopped breathing as the adrenaline built up in her body. She wanted to flee, but she knew she had to stay. She had told Andres she *hated* public speaking, how could he forget?

"Hmm, I'm just..." she started desperately trying to find the words. *Any* words.

"I feel that..."

She felt the stems of the flower bouquet break in her sweaty hands as she turned to Andres with a wide smile. "I feel the same way."

The crowd stayed quiet, followed by a lonely clap from the back of the chapel.

Melissa didn't have to turn to see Hugo's mocking face.

Luckily, her embarrassment was short-lived as the vicar continued the ceremony. To Melissa's surprise, Hugo didn't take any part in the official ceremony and didn't say a word when the vicar asked the crowd to speak up if they had any reason why the marriage should not go ahead. Melissa didn't expect him to protest but would have imagined him to comment, especially since he had deliberately asked her to stay away from his brother. She was even more surprised at his swift departure before they had even finished walking down the aisle.

A moment of disappointment washed over her the minute she heard the double doors slam shut, but she kept the smile on her face as she walked through the confetti rain hand in hand with her new husband.

Cheers and merry laughter followed them outside and they entered the black Rolls Royce Phantom that Andres had insisted on having. Andres opened the door for her and waited for the driver to assist him into the other side. Melissa looked at her newly-wedded husband and observed his calmness, despite clearly displaying his condition in front of all the guests.

"I'm so happy to see you like this, Andres. You look so happy," Melissa said with a smile as she patted his leg.

Andres huffed and pushed her hand away. "What do you expect me to do? Cry?"

Melissa frowned at his outburst but remained silent throughout the entire journey home.

She hoped Andres had been nervous about the wedding and would calm down once they got back home, but she couldn't have been more wrong.

As they arrived, Melissa got out of the car and walked to the other side to help Andres into his chair, but he pushed her away with force. "I don't need your help, go inside!"

Melissa stepped back to keep her balance and tilted her head, confused by his sudden mood change. "But, Andres, I want to help, it's not a problem for me at all."

Andres laughed with bitterness. "Well in that case, just do as any paid help does and jump when I tell you to!"

Melissa jerked her head up. "This isn't funny, Andres!"

He waited until the driver bowed his head and drove away.

"It's not supposed to be funny at all, Melissa, just get inside! I've got more important things to do!" Andres barked, pulling a silver flask from his pocket.

The strong smell of whiskey filled the air around them and Melissa sighed.

"I don't think you should drink with your medication," she said.

"Why? Because I might not be able to drive or have sex on our wedding night?" Andres retorted, glugging the alcohol and burping aloud. "Oh, I forgot. I can't do any of those things anymore, ever!"

Melissa glared at him with a knitted brow. "I don't understand, Andres. I thought you were doing great with your physiotherapist and all the staff who are helping you adjust to the new circumstances."

He took another long sip and carefully closed the flask, putting it back into the inner pocket of his jacket.

"You nailed it, Melissa. I'm adjusting very well with the assistance of *paid* help, which *you* are now effectively part of, so I strongly advise you to leave those smart comments outside and follow my instructions if you want me to pay the repayments of your family home, which your father wouldn't have lost if he hadn't stupidly paid for the impulse purchases of a woman who had slept with half of the town in the meantime!"

Melissa paused as Andres' icy words stabbed her heart. "That's not true!"

Andres scoffed. "You don't believe me? Ask anyone in town. A lot of things changed whilst you played career woman in London, Melissa. Oh, and that reminds me, you better start making arrangements with your boss to relocate here."

Melissa stared at him. "What are you talking about?"

"Well, you can't expect me to stay in London, can you?" Andres said, wide-eyed. "The house is certainly not equipped for wheelchairs and I'm too tired of the busy life in the city anyway, so I have decided to stay here – with you."

"But you promised that I could continue working!" Melissa cried, holding back the tears that were dangerously reaching the surface.

"That's right, but I never said you could stay *in London* to work, did

I?" Andres corrected. "I have arranged a laptop for you to work in your room a couple of days a week, and I expect you to explain to your boss that you won't be working full-time anymore as you need to take care of your sick husband."

Melissa huffed and folded her arms. "But all the big portfolios need daily attention. What am I supposed to do with them?"

"Don't take that tone with me, Melissa, you know what you were getting yourself into when you asked me to marry you to cover your father's debts!" Andres barked.

"I never asked you to cover the debts, Andres, *you* proposed to *me* and suggested it yourself!"

"Well, you didn't exactly say no to me at any point. On the contrary, it seemed to be the only way to get you to marry me at all."

Melissa shook her head. "That's not true and you know it."

"Really?" Andres said, tilting his head to the side. "Think about it, would you have *actually* married me if I didn't offer to cover your father's debts?"

Melissa stayed quiet as the realisation hit her.

Andres watched her pale face turn pink and scoffed. "I didn't think so, Melissa. After all, you are not in love with me. You just *used* me to get what you wanted."

Hot tears surfaced in Melissa's eyes and her voice broke. "Why are you doing this? Why did you propose to me if you knew I never wanted marriage?"

Andres stared at his manicured nails, uninterested. "Well, I need a presentable companion to accompany me to events and so on, and since you were so *willing* to do it, well… you do the maths."

"You could have had anyone, why me?" Melissa asked through sobs.

"Are you joking?" Andres questioned. "Since my accident, only prostitutes are willing to satisfy me, but that's too expensive, whereas you, my dear, you sold yourself cheap." He eyed her from head to toe. "Not to say I would have paid a penny more.."

Melissa followed his eyes and covered her low-cut dress with her hands. She felt exposed and ridiculed under his hateful gaze.

Andres glared at Melissa once more and wheeled inside.

"I don't care if you freeze to death outside as long as you don't leave the estate," he said over his shoulder. "So, don't even *think* about trying to escape. I have twenty-four-hour security on site to look after you – I wouldn't want anything bad to happen to Mrs Ferrero now, would I?"

Andres disappeared inside, and when Melissa heard the front door close, she raced to the main gate and tried to yank it open. She stumbled in her wedding dress when a dark figure approached her.

"*Madam*, you need to go inside. It's freezing," one of the security guards ordered.

"No, I certainly won't go inside, open the gate or leave!"

"I have strict instructions from Mr Ferrero to keep you inside the estate."

"I don't care what instructions you've been given from Mr Ferrero, open the gate, now!"

The security guard tried to grab her by the shoulders, but Melissa dodged him just in time. "Don't you ever try to touch me again!"

"Mr Ferrero said you would react this way, so he asked me to give you this," the security guard said, pulling out a piece of paper from his pocket.

Melissa took the paper and read the short note.

"*My dearest Melissa, if you don't stop making a scene, I will have no choice but to call the bank and ask them to auction your father's house at the first opportunity. I already have a couple of investor friends who are interested in the property, so I'm sure selling the house within a few weeks wouldn't be a problem. Think about it next time you want to disobey me."*

Melissa's stomach cramped with nausea and her heart filled with a sinking dread as the security guard escorted her back inside the house. She wandered into the dining area to see Andres at the table with a plate of food in front of him.

"There you are, my dear, would you like to eat our wedding dinner now, or shall I ask for it to be delivered to your room?" Andres asked with a smile as if he had forgotten their previous conversation.

Melissa eyed the table and noticed that only one table set had been arranged. Andres followed her gaze and continued.

"Apologies, I removed your table set for I assumed you wouldn't want to present yourself with puffy eyes at our wedding dinner."

Melissa's stomach growled, but she refused to eat in front of him under any circumstances. "Food upstairs is fine."

Andres wiped his face with a napkin and sipped his red wine. "Very well, I think Mrs Whittle should be free to show you to your room. It's upstairs next to mine, you can't miss it."

Andres returned to his dinner and Melissa headed for the staircase when Mrs Whittle appeared from nowhere.

"Good evening, Melissa, you must be exhausted after such a long day! Come on, let me show you to your room."

Melissa followed Mrs Whittle to her new prison cell and stepped inside.

"I've laid fresh linen and hung your clothing in the closet," she said, pointing to the wardrobe. "All the toiletries and your make-up are in the bathroom, but if you would rather apply your make-up in the natural light, I can arrange a table to be set in front of the window.

"That's fine, thank you, Mrs Whittle," Melissa replied without emotion. "I don't use that much make-up anyway."

Mrs Whittle shook her head. "Mr Ferrero fancies his wife to wear her make-up around the house and always look put together in case of visitors."

Melissa rolled her eyes. "Ok, give me a schedule of visitors and I'll make sure I'm always presentable for when they arrive."

"Honestly, *Madam,* I don't think sarcasm is the way forward. My boy has suffered enough in this life, and since you're only here for the *money*, I suggest you comply with his wishes. It's the least you can do."

Mrs Whittle glared at Melissa before she turned and left the room. As her footsteps faded from earshot, Melissa slumped onto her new bed and let the tears flow.

"What have I done?"

8 CHAPTER

A few hours later, Melissa's sobs dried out and she slipped out of her wedding dress and freshened up in the en-suite. She searched for her oversized cotton t-shirt when Andres wheeled into the room without knocking.

"Excuse me, is it too much trouble to knock?" Melissa snapped, covering herself with the morning gown she had left on the bed.

Andres' mouth quivered into a mischievous smile. "Why on earth would I miss my wife taking off her clothes? You're not the worst sight for sore eyes, but you *definitely* need some work around the hip area – they are quite wide for your height, which makes you look like a minion."

Melissa blushed with embarrassment and tightened the rope around her waist. She clenched her fists and steadied her breath, looking Andres straight in the eye.

"Go away, Andres, haven't you done enough?"

Andres burst into laughter. "Oh, Melissa, you have no idea! But don't worry, you will find out soon enough."

Andres turned his chair around to leave but halted before the door.

"I'm sorry you would rather I left you alone on your wedding night. I would have been more than happy to climb into your bed, but you've left leave me cold in every way," he said, eyeing her simple morning gown. "Even if I don't wish to sleep with you, I still expect you to wear the sexy night garment in the closet. It's the least you can do, don't you think?"

When Andres finally wheeled out of the room and closed the door behind him, Melissa exhaled and opened her fists.

She tried to let Andres' insults go over her head, but it proved difficult as she noticed her wide hips in the full-length mirror. Melissa sighed and crawled between the fresh linen sheets, hoping that she wouldn't have to interact with Andres too much. The house had been built big enough to avoid him, but soon after she fell into a restless sleep, her hope shattered.

"Melissa, I need water!" Andres yelled from the next room. "Fetch me a glass, will you?"

Melissa huffed and rubbed her eyes.

"For fuck's sake, come on, Melissa, I don't have all night, I'm thirsty!" Andres shouted.

Melissa slipped into her sleepers and morning gown and entered the room by using the joint entrance connecting the two rooms.

"May I help you?" Melissa questioned, glaring at her brute of a husband.

Andres lay topless in his king-sized bed with messy hair and a five o'clock shadow across his jawline. His pyjama bottoms drooped so low that Melissa would have seen everything if he moved as much as an inch. Melissa eyed his athletic figure and kept a blank expression.

"You like what you see?" Andres teased, winking at her as if he had noticed her curiosity.

Melissa shrugged. "Nothing I haven't seen before."

"Oh, is that so? And here I thought you hadn't dated anyone since your unsuccessful experience at university."

Melissa kept quiet even though she wondered how Andres knew about her relationship with James, a fellow student who she had met years ago.

It had been the last year of university when she had met James, who had asked her out a couple of times. Having been a virgin and curious about sex at that time, she had slept with him after their second date. Their relationship would have continued longer without a doubt, but Melissa relocated to London after university to pursue her career in accounting and James left for Scotland to work in the family business.

Her thoughts were cut short when Mrs Whittle burst into the room.

"What an earth is going on here?" she barked.

Melissa and Andres stared at the open door with bulging eyes.

Andres burst into a pretentious cry. "I woke up thirsty, so I simply asked Melissa to bring me a glass of water, but she refused and made fun of me for not being able to do it myself!" Andres lied, covering his face with his palms.

Melissa scoffed with incredulousness and Mrs Whittle glowered at her. "Young lady, I appreciate that you are now the woman of the house, but I must express my deep disappointment in your uncouth manner towards your husband! You need to make sure he has everything he needs, not taunt him!"

Melissa opened her mouth to protest, but Andres's challenging expression told her she would lose the battle no matter what she said.

"My apologies, Andres, I didn't realise our chat kept me away from attending to your needs," Melissa said through gritted teeth. She bowed and hurried passed Mrs Whittle. "I'll be right back."

Melissa dashed down to the kitchen and filled a clean glass with water. She leaned on one of the kitchen counters and took a deep breath, wishing she could rewind to the moment Andres asked her to marry him.

When she returned upstairs, she placed the glass onto Andres' nightstand as Mrs Whittle tucked him in.

"Is there anything else you might need?" Melissa asked.

Andres grinned at Mrs Whittle. "No, I think I have everything I need as long as I have this superwoman next to me."

Andres tickled Mrs Whittle's large hips and she slapped his hand, giggling at the same time. "Oh, you are such a charmer, Mr Ferrero, just like your father before he met the late Mrs Ferrero."

Melissa rolled her eyes and yawned. "Ok, then if you'll excuse me, I'm going back to bed."

Melissa crept back into bed when Andres called her a few minutes later.

"Melissa, I dropped my duvet, I'm cold!"

Melissa grumbled under her breath, but she couldn't afford to disobey him again. She *needed* to keep her family home.

Without a word, she got out of bed yet again and entered Andres' room.

***

After a week of living in the Ferrero Mansion, Melissa felt exhausted with dark circles around her eyes. She hadn't weighed herself, but her reflection told her that she was doing exactly what Andres had suggested - lose weight.

As a sudden wisp of cold air burst into the room, Melissa sighed as she prepared herself for the breakfast Andres expected her to have with him every morning. She snuggled deeper into her morning gown, which covered the ridiculously short garment Andres expected her to wear at night.

Melissa sneezed and rubbed her blocked nose.

"Great, catching a cold is the last thing I need right now," she thought when she heard a voice next door.

"Melissa, I need my morning paper, now!"

Melissa rolled her eyes and got up from her seat.

"On my way!" she yelled through the door and made her way downstairs.

Melissa grabbed the folded Financial Times from the front porch and took a moment to admire the gorgeous line of flowers leading to the front gate.

Even if there wasn't twenty-four-hour security around the mansion, there was no life for Melissa outside of the gates if she would lose her precious family home.

She gave a loud sigh and returned inside.

"It's about time, where were you? I have been waiting forever!"

"It took me literally two minutes to run downstairs to pick up your paper," Melissa said and handed it over.

"On second thoughts, I'm not that interested in reading the paper today," Andres said, tossing it on the floor and smiling at her.

Melissa gritted her teeth but remained calm. It wasn't the first or the last morning Andres had sent her to pick him up a paper he didn't read or a glass of water he didn't drink.

"Wouldn't it be easier for any of your other staff members working on the ground floor to fetch the paper for you to read whilst having breakfast?" Melissa suggested practically.

"I see, a couple of nights in the mansion surrounded by staff and you already feel lazy to put any effort in for the money I'm paying for the piece of crap you call a house!"

His unjustified words stabbed deep, but Melissa kept quiet. Crying in front of him wasn't an option.

"If you don't need anything else, I'll just…"

"No time, the breakfast is served now, get downstairs. I'll be right there."

"But I just have to finish my…"

"I said, no time for that," Andres interjected and motioned her to leave the room.

Melissa huffed and marched out of the room to the staircase.

She hadn't had time to finish her makeup or change her clothing, which she was sure Andres wouldn't miss a chance to comment on, so she sat silently at the table and waited for Andres to wheel into the room. He stunk of cologne, and his freshly-shaven jawline told her that he had taken his time showing whilst Melissa had rushed downstairs for nothing.

"I can see that your lack of effort doesn't only concern your husband. You look hideous."

"I'm sorry, I expected to have more time in the morning instead of running your errands."

Andres wheeled to the head of the table and folded a white napkin onto his lap. "Well, that simply means that you should wake up earlier."

Melissa launched up from her chair. "I wake up before six every morning after having served you throughout the night. When do you expect me to sleep?!"

"Sit down."

"I will not!"

"I said, sit down and stop this scene!" Andres snarled and slammed his hands on the wooden table.

His sudden reaction startled Melissa, and she sat down again, looking into the emptiness before her. Andres didn't speak; instead, he enjoyed his breakfast without reading his morning paper.

Melissa held herself for as long as she could, but when she saw Andres taking his last bite and finishing his morning coffee, she stood up. "May I excuse myself now?"

"Do whatever you like."

If only

Melissa hurried to her room and slammed the door behind her. She quickly dialled her mother's mobile, but it went straight to voicemail as it had ever since she had gotten home from the wedding.

She had been worried at first, but as soon as she had received a simple WhatsApp message to let her know that Andres had paid her mother to go on an expensive holiday in the French Riviera, it made sense; another one of Andres' ways to make her life miserable and ensure that she remained idle in the mansion without company.

Melissa tossed her mobile across the bed and sat down in front of her work desk.

She checked her inbox and watched as it filled with high-priority emails, but it would be impossible to respond to them all knowing that Andres would "need" her at any given moment.

At first, she had played with the idea of continuing working full-time despite Andres' demands, but after each day passed, it looked more difficult, and she didn't want the company to suffer because of her. She dialled a Teams call to her boss.

"Melissa, this is a pleasant surprise! I've been meaning to call you. How have you been? I haven't seen you online for days now," her boss said, answering after the first ring.

"I know, Jason, I have been busy," Melissa responded.

She didn't want to make the call any longer than necessary.

"What's up, Melissa? You know I need your response to tons of emails this week. Your honeymoon is over, my dear, but I can't afford to lose any clients because of your romantic getaway in the countryside."

If only he knew.

"Well, actually this is something I wanted to speak to you about. I don't think I should continue managing the biggest accounts, so I would like to transfer them to someone who would be able to give them the attention they need."

"What? But you love working on the biggest accounts, you've earned them with your hard work!"

Melissa felt a lump in her throat and hot tears surfacing. "I know, Jason, but my circumstances have changed since we last time spoke."

"What do you mean? You've just got married, it's hardly a life sentence."

"I know, but my husband needs me on daily basis quite a lot and I cannot let my personal life intervene with business, it wouldn't be fair on everyone else in the office."

"Is this about the comment I just made about losing clients? If it is Melissa, you know I was only joking!"

"I know, but there is a seed of truth there, Jason. We both know it."

"But the biggest accounts make over 70% of your whole portfolio! You really want to give them away?"

"Yes."

"Right, ok, but you do realise that we don't have that many smaller accounts, don't you? Every client needs the attention on a regular basis, even if the revenue from the account is less?"

Melissa nodded. "I will do everything I can to give them the attention they need."

A short silence ensued as Melissa watched his boss sink into his thoughts.

"Melissa, I do hope you know this certainly won't accelerate your career, on the contrary, you might end up being stuck where you are for years… or worse. Are you sure about this?"

"I'm positive," Melissa said.

"Well then, I guess there is nothing I can do to persuade you. Let me speak with HR and get back to you. I have never had a part-time employee, so I need to seek consultation. Shall we speak in person next time you're in the city?"

"Look, can you just finish the paperwork for me? I don't know when I will be in the city next time."

"What do you mean you don't know; you still work with us right?"

"Yes, but my husband now takes the priority."

"Jeez, Melissa, I knew you were in love but to go to this length… and I don't have a problem with people working from home time to time, but you will end up tossing your career away."

"I know…"

Whilst Melissa listened to him carefully, she wasn't able to break the details to her boss, so she hid behind the excuse of taking care of her sick husband, just like Andres had predicted.

***

A couple of nights after the wedding, Melissa enjoyed the warmth of the fireplace and the escape of her book when Andres wheeled into the room.

"We will have guests today, so I expect you to make an extra effort with your appearance," he demanded.

"No problem, just let me know what time you expect me down," Melissa said and kept reading.

A dark shadow descended over his beautiful face. "Ok, good. Oh, and I want to see something sexy on you, not this office look you keep trying to pull off every day. It's boring!"

Andres eyed her simple pencil skirt and cream Cashmere cardigan paired with the pumps she had left on the floor in front of the sofa.

Melissa sighed and turned the page of her book. "Of course, Andres, I wouldn't want to embarrass you in any way."

"God, even your *voice* is boring!" Andres exclaimed. "I feel like I'm living with a ghost."

Melissa wanted to scream and shout at Andres and blame him for her behaviour, but she knew it would only backfire, so she bit her lip and continued to hide her frustration.

"Apologies, Andres, I will try to be more entertaining in the future."

"Well, it might work in our favour tonight," Andres said, rubbing his chin. "Hugo will be bored to death and will likely disappear again."

Andres turned to leave, but the sound of Hugo's name filled Melissa with butterflies. The blood froze in her veins, and she lowered the book from her face.

"I'm sorry, who did you say your guest was?"

"My brother and his girlfriend, I assume. One of the many, anyway," Andres replied, scoffing and leaving the living room.

Although the fire danced in the fireplace and heated the room, a cold shiver surged down Melissa's spine. She hadn't seen Hugo since his brief appearance at their wedding, and she wondered how her life would have panned out if she had listened to his demand to cancel the dinner date with his brother.

She would have kept her happiness, but surely lost her father's house. Would it have been worth it?

The idea of seeing Hugo again filled her with childish excitement, but the thought of meeting his girlfriend made her stomach knot together with a sense of darkness she couldn't explain.

That evening, Melissa prepared herself more thoroughly than ever before.

She bathed in essential oils, washed her hair with volumizing shampoo, and applied a full face of make-up that would have made her mother proud. She had still left her skin bare with a natural glow and focused on intensifying her blue eyes and plump lips.

It'll do, she thought and turned around to get dressed.

Melissa changed into a long-sleeve sequin dress that hugged her curves and displayed just enough neck and collarbone. Its emerald glow complemented her skin and reminded her of the forest behind the Ferrero mansion she so much admired from her window. She had considered dressing in black just to piss Andres off, but she wanted to keep her pride in front of Hugo. There was no point parading her failed marriage in front of anyone, especially Hugo.

Melissa sighed as she looked into the full-length and stared at her figure. She had lost weight since the wedding, particularly from her waist and thighs, leaving her with even more of an hourglass shape and fuller breasts. Most women spend millions to get a body like hers, but she didn't want to give Andres more of a reason to ogle at her just to criticise, so she stuck to simple bras without padding.

But tonight, she had slipped into a push-up piece from Victoria's Secret's catalogue and enjoyed the way the delicate fabric rubbed against her bare skin. The colour of the satin matched her dress, and she almost felt disappointed not to have anyone to share the intimate moment with. The sad thought was too much to bear; a tiny tear emerged from the corner of her eye as Andres called her from downstairs.

"Melissa, the guests are here! Get down here, *now*!"

Melissa glanced at the clock on the wall and frowned. The guests had arrived half an hour early, but it was pointless arguing with Andres, so she slipped into her black high heels and made her way downstairs.

"About time!" Andres barked, yanking Melissa closer to him. "You're always late, trying to embarrass me!"

Andres wore a plain black tux and had a golden Rolex around his wrist. His hair had been combed back, and when his sulky expression disappeared, he looked *exactly* like Hugo.

Melissa avoided his touch and Andres scowled.

"What do you think you are doing? Come here, I don't want to say this again!"

Without a word, Melissa shuffled closer and allowed him to embrace her from her waist. She forced a wide smile and welcomed the guests.

9 CHAPTER

"Good evening, family."

Against her will, Melissa melted at Hugo's masculine voice as he emerged from the doorway and shook his wet leather coat.

"Hugo, for Christ's sake! You know how difficult it is for me to get around on a wet floor!" Andres barked.

Hugo raised an eyebrow at Andres as if to reconsider whether to enter the house at all.

Melissa panicked and glanced between Hugo and Andres. She didn't want Hugo to go and leave her curiosity unsatisfied, so she touched Andres' cheek and turned to him. "Sweetheart, give the guests room to breathe. I'm sure Mrs Whittle is more than capable of taking care of any water on the floor whilst we are dining."

Andres narrowed his eyes. "Well, that shouldn't be her job."

Melissa burst into unnatural laughter. "Oh, *darling*, it's pouring cats and dogs outside and you know how efficient she can be. I wouldn't worry about it too much."

Hugo lowered his eyebrows and closed the door. "Are you talking about old Mrs Whittle?"

Andres nodded. "Yes, I rehired her and offered her a room so she could spend her retirement years here as a friend rather than a member of staff."

Hugo clapped his hands together. "Well, look at that, Brother, I'm surprised you were able to lure Mean Mrs Whittle back, I thought we'd had enough of her pulling our ears every time Mum wasn't around."

"Well, that might be *your* experience with her, but she always treated me with respect."

Hugo grinned. "Naturally, as you were her favourite."

"Nothing more than you were for our mother."

Hugo tensed and spoke through gritted teeth. "I was never Mum's favourite, and you know it, we just happened to have the same interests in life, that's all."

Hugo and Andres scowled at each other and Melissa worried that one of them would start a fight.

"Hugo, I thought you came with someone?" Melissa said, trying to change the subject.

She wasn't eager to meet anyone Hugo had brought with him but felt obliged to distract the brothers to allow the evening to continue. Hugo's eyes widened and he grabbed the door handle.

"Oh, dear God, Gloria!"

As Hugo stuck his head out the door to summon his girlfriend, Andres turned to Melissa and scrunched up his face. "I appreciate your intention to play happy families, but it's Hugo's fault I'm confined to this bloody chair! If it wasn't for him, I wouldn't have laid eyes on you and you would have lost your precious family house! So, whatever you're doing, stop it!"

Andres turned around as a tall woman sauntered into the house. Her heels clattered against the floor and her tiny red dress was so vulgarly short that it made Melissa feel like a church girl on Sunday. Appreciation glowed in Andres' eyes, and Melissa's mood sank even lower.

The woman crouched before Andres and smiled. "You must be Andres; Hugo has told me so much about you."

Andres remained silent and stared at the woman's chest.

"Oh, pardon me, this dress is *killing* me for sliding lower and lower all the time!" she said but didn't make an effort to pull the dress up.

"No reason to apologise for such a lovely view," Andres said, catching Melissa's eye. "It's such an honour to have you here Miss…?"

"Garcia. Gloria Garcia! It's so nice to meet you," she replied, reaching out for a handshake.

Andres took her hand and kissed her tanned skin.

"Trust me, the *pleasure* is all mine."

Gloria giggled and Hugo re-emerged from the door without shaking his wet jacket this time.

"Have you all got acquainted?" he asked, hanging his and Gloria's fur coat on the hooks.

"I certainly have," Andres said with a smile. "But I don't think Melissa has had the courtesy to do so yet. Come on, sweetheart, there is no reason to feel second best."

Andres pushed Melissa forward and she blushed with embarrassment, but she held her head high and offered her hand to Gloria. "Nice to meet you, Miss Garcia, welcome to Ferrero Mansion."

"Oh, come here, you!" Gloria chirped, and she pulled Melissa into a bear hug.

Melissa raised her eyebrows with surprise and her stomach twisted with unease as Gloria's braless breasts pressed against her chest, but she couldn't afford to embarrass a guest with Andres eying her every move.

Melissa patted Gloria's naked back and said, "Well, it's truly a pleasure."

"Oh, call me Gloria as I'm certainly going to call you Melissa!" she exclaimed, pulling away. "God, your skin looks amazing! How do you get it to look so smooth?"

"It's called fresh air, Gloria, a rarity in London," Hugo said, pulling Melissa into a formal hug. "It's good to see you, Melissa, long time and *so many* things have changed."

Hugo's five o'clock shadow rubbed against her cheek, but she fought the need to scratch her skin. She looked for a hidden message in Hugo's expression when they parted, but he remained neutral towards her and beamed at Gloria who stood next to him. When their bodies parted, Melissa felt sudden cold air on her skin and shivered. She *needed* him to lay his eyes on *her* and bring back the warmth she so much craved after wandering the endless corridors of Ferrero Mansion for months on end, alone, hollow as a ghost.

Nonsense.

Hugo wrapped his arm around Gloria's waist, and she giggled at his touch. Melissa's heart twinged with jealousy, but the corner of her lip twitched into a genuine smile as she followed Andres to the dining room.

She would be so much easier to hate if she hadn't been so nice to her.

"Mrs Whittle, looking better than ever," Hugo greeted as he grabbed a glass of champagne from the waitress' open tray.

Mrs Whittle nodded but didn't say a word until Andres wheeled next to her. She placed her hand protectively on his shoulder to show everyone where her loyalty lay.

"It's delightful to have you stop by, Mr Ferrero," Mrs Whittle said to Hugo. "Only several months after your last visit. I wonder what you have been up to that has been so much more important than your family."

Melissa's eyes bulged at the poorly hidden sarcasm in her tone, and her heart rate tripled. Hugo gulped the rest of his champagne and raised the empty glass towards the chubby housekeeper.

"Better late than never."

Mrs Whittle snorted loudly and looked at Andres. "The dinner is served. Whenever you are ready."

Hugo and Gloria clasped hands and Melissa pursed her lips at their intimate gesture. They ambled over to the dining table and Andres gestured for Gloria to sit next to him in Melissa's usual seat.

Melissa bit her tongue and sat in the guest chair opposite Hugo.

Andres and Gloria maintained light conversation throughout the appetisers and Hugo glugged a few glasses of wine and whiskey down his throat. He swirled the brown liquid in his short glass and avoided Melissa like a plague.

"Veal and roasted potatoes with red wine sauce," the waitress announced as she placed a hot plate in front of Melissa.

"Oh, Judith, I'm sorry but as you know, I don't eat meat," Melissa whispered, handing the plate back.

Judith furrowed her brow and glanced at Andres. "But, Madam, Mr Ferrero asked for veal for you."

A heavy silence filled the dining room and Melissa shuffled her feet under the table.

Andres scoffed. "Jesus, Melissa, can't you make an exception this time? Everyone is waiting to eat!"

Melissa lowered her voice. "Andres, you know I don't eat meat, how can you forget?"

"My god, Melissa, really? You want us to argue in front of our guests?" Andres snapped, slamming his palm on the table.

Melissa gulped and forced a smile. "Of course not, darling."

Melissa turned back to her meal and cut the veal into tiny bits. Andres watched her and grew impatient.

"Are you going to play with your food forever or actually eat it?" Andres taunted, looking at Gloria for approval, but she glanced at the chandelier above the table and stayed out of the conversation.

"Of course I'm going to eat it," Melissa replied, forcing back the tears.

She took a deep breath and closed her eyes as she brought the fork to her mouth.

"Actually, I haven't eaten meat for a long time and that looks delicious. Do you mind, Brother, if I switch my meal with your wife's?"

Andres turned to Hugo and scowled. "What do you mean, Brother? You asked for white fish, so you've been given white fish."

Hugo shrugged and wrapped one arm around Gloria. "I have a feeling I might need the extra protein tonight, otherwise someone is going to be disappointed."

Hugo winked at Gloria, and she burst into laughter.

"You dirty man, Hugo Ferrero!" she cried, smacking his tight chest.

Andres smiled. "Very well then, you love birds."

Andres made a gesture and the waitress switched Hugo's plate with Melissa's.

Melissa felt grateful for Hugo coming to the rescue, but his excuse crushed her appetite, so she forced the food down and tried not to bring it back up.

The conversation returned to normal, and Gloria asked multiple questions about the estate and their childhood without bringing attention to the accident. As Andres treated Gloria like the most interesting thing in the room, Melissa could relax for a short while and enjoy her evening away from the microscope, but she would have enjoyed her dinner even more if Hugo hadn't been opposite her the entire time.

Once the waitress cleared the dinner plates, they finished with Mrs

Whittle's famous sticky toffee cake when Andres turned to Gloria. "Would you care to join me for a coffee and liqueur in the salon, Gloria?"

Gloria grinned and stood from Melissa's seat. "I would be honoured, handsome."

The two of them left the dining room and left Melissa and Hugo alone.

After a few moments of an unnatural silence between them, Melissa cleared her throat and got to her feet to collect the dessert plates. Hugo finished his fifth glass of Jack Daniels when he glowered at Melissa.

"How could you be so greedy, *woman?*"

Melissa jerked her head up and knitted her brow. "I beg your pardon?"

"You heard me. What made you so greedy? What did he promise you, money, clothes? And don't you dare insult me by telling me you simply fell in love with him the second you saw him, I don't buy that shit!"

Melissa piled the dessert plates together and tensed her shoulders.

"I don't think it's any of your business."

Melissa reached for Hugo's plate, but he grabbed her wrist and forced her to stop.

"I told you to stay away from my brother. Only a fool would tie themselves to a bitter bastard," Hugo hissed through gritted teeth. "Or someone extremely greedy and calculative."

"Well, you seem to have already decided which one I am."

Hugo slammed his fist on the table and leaned toward Melissa. "You are such a bitch who deserves all the bad things you are about to experience with my brother! You hear me?!"

Melissa wrenched her hand from his grip and caressed her sensitive skin. "That will be my decision then, don't you think?"

Hugo shook his head and eyed her with disgust. "What kind of woman takes advantage of a helpless man in a wheelchair? He won't be even able to satisfy you in bed!"

"That's none of your business!" Melissa retorted, eyeing the doorway in case Andres heard.

She didn't mind him seeing her having a conversation with his brother, but the topic would no doubt raise questions Melissa wasn't prepared to answer.

"Andres wouldn't have even *looked* at you if he could walk, I hope you know that!"

"I know that," Melissa replied calmly as she finished collecting the plates.

"Well, you both certainly deserve each other then!"

Hugo stood abruptly and launched his whiskey glass against the wall. The glass shattered and one of his mother's paintings slid to the floor.

Melissa quickly reversed into the farthest corner when Mrs Whittle waddled into the room.

"Mr Ferrero, that's enough of your drunken behaviour for tonight or I will call the police and you'll spend your night at the station!" she barked.

Hugo wiped his nose with his sleeve and smiled. "Old Mean Mrs Whittle, always there to save the day! What would my mother have done without you?"

Melissa could hear the sarcasm in his voice, and she relaxed for a second knowing that she wouldn't be in the spotlight anymore.

Mrs Whittle huffed and turned to Melissa. "Mrs Ferrero, please leave the room and let me pour a strong coffee for this *Red Head*."

Melissa nodded and hurried to the door, leaving the dessert plates on the corner of the table.

"Good, run whilst you can, you greedy bitch!" Hugo called after her. "I hope there will be nothing left of you when my brother is done with you, you hear me?"

Melissa ignored Hugo's cruel words and made her way to the salon, but when she opened the door, her heart dropped. Andres and Gloria were sitting on a sofa and Andres had placed his hand on her thigh close to the edge of her dress. She didn't seem to be uncomfortable with the idea at all. On the contrary, she giggled and placed her hand on top of his when she saw Melissa.

"Oh, Melissa, my apologies, Andres was just trying to…" Gloria struggled, but Andres came to the rescue.

"Calm down, Princess," Andres said, patting her leg and turning to Melissa. "*Darling*, I know you are working hard to ensure your body is in its best shape, but you can't blame a sick man for enjoying the simple joys of life."

Andres rubbed Gloria's long legs and Melissa ignored the insult, forcing a smile.

"That's great, I'm happy you have found a new interest in your life, Andres. Anyone up for more coffee?" she asked, but before Andres or Gloria could respond, she turned and grabbed the door handle. "I'll get some."

Melissa slammed the salon door and dug her nails into her palms. She flared her nostrils with rage and charged towards the entrance hall.

The coffee could wait.

She swung open the front door and inhaled the cold air, closing the door behind her and shivering against the hard wood.

Just a moment to cool off and I'll be better than new, she thought and breathed deep.

Hugo had been right yet so *wrong* at the same time. Melissa knew she had taken advantage of Andres's proposal, but she hadn't been driven by *greed*. In fact, she didn't want *any* of the luxuries her role as Andres's wife offered her. It had been the love for her father and the family home she simply refused to lose. She hadn't been left with much of a choice as time had been against her. Miraculously, Andres's proposal had come at the best time.

If only she could make Hugo see the situation from her point of view, but she knew he wasn't interested in hearing a sleazy, sob story. It was *his brother* after all, and regardless of the bad stigma that circled them, they were twin brothers and he was looking after him, paying for the house where Melissa was solely a guest for the time being.

As Melissa lost herself within her thoughts, the door cracked open and Gloria stepped outside.

"It's a beautiful evening, isn't it?" she said, gazing up at the dark sky.

Melissa quickly wiped her tears and sniffled. "Yes, you can see the stars very clearly in this part of England. I can't remember the sky being this clear in London."

Gloria eyed Melissa with curiosity. "You used to work in London, didn't you?"

Melissa nodded. "Since I graduated from university."

"Interesting," Gloria replied and examined her further. "What did you major in?"

"Mainly accounting and maths," Melissa said with a shy smile. "I love numbers."

"That's so cool!" Gloria exclaimed, exposing her perfect teeth through a genuine grin.

Melissa cleared her throat and remembered her position as hostess of the evening. "So, what about you Miss Gar– I mean *Gloria*."

"I'm a biologist. "

Melissa blinked in disbelief. "That's impressive!"

Gloria laughed. "Tell me about it! I'm the first graduate in my family. That's how I met Hugo."

"Oh," Melissa said, carefully controlling her curiosity.

"It was definitely a *wow* moment," she went on, smiling at the memory. "Chemistry at first sight."

Melissa clenched her jaw and controlled her breathing. A shot of jealousy twisted her stomach as she eyed Gloria up and down. She had the looks *and* the brains.

Melissa glanced down at her simple dress and felt ridiculous; it had looked sexy just moments before Gloria had strutted inside the house. How silly she had been to even *think* she could compete with any of Hugo's girlfriends.

"Anyway, I think we should go back in… our boys are arguing in Andres' office," Gloria said, biting her lip with apology.

"Oh, I hope it's nothing serious," Melissa replied, taking control of herself again, and the two of them hurried back inside.

As Melissa and Gloria rushed through the entrance hall, the sound of glass shattering echoed from Andres' office.

"You must be out of your mind, Brother!" Hugo roared. "I wouldn't do it even if you *paid* me!"

Gloria touched Melissa's shoulder from behind. "Should we go in?"

Melissa winced and patted Gloria's palm. "I don't think we should intervene any further. Perhaps we should go to the salon and have another cup of tea?"

Gloria nodded, but when they turned away from Andres' office, a loud *thump* caught their attention, followed by Andres laughing with malice. "Well, suit yourself, I'll have it my way with or *without you!*"

The office fell silent, and Gloria glanced at Melissa with wide eyes.

"Follow me!" Melissa whispered, terrified that Andres would catch them eavesdropping.

Melissa led Gloria to the salon where Mrs Whittle had conveniently left a hot pot of tea and some chocolates on display. They made themselves comfortable and continued light conversation about Melissa's career.

Melissa didn't expect Gloria to be so interested in listening to her, but she appreciated it after weeks of being silenced by Andres. She was surprised to discover that Gloria was an excellent listener and seemed interested in hearing her talk and express her opinions. Her energy was contagious and came with a hint of masculinity, which could explain why she had such an effortless relationship with Hugo. They seemed to understand each other without words.

"Melissa, I hope you don't think I'm taking advantage of our evening, but I'm a shareholder of a global company that specialises in importing South American goods here in the UK. But we are yet to find an accountant who could take over the company accounts."

"Oh?" Melissa said, holding her breath.

"I know you're not a freelancer, but if you're happy to give me your company's contact details, I would be delighted to get in touch with your boss about opening an account with you. Does that sound like something you would be interested in?"

Despite Melissa's jealousy, her heart rate increased with excitement and she illuminated inside. "I would be honoured, Gloria."

Gloria grinned. "It's settled then, if you pass me your company's contact details, I'll try to set up something for early next week."

Melissa scribbled the office landline number onto a white napkin as she feared she wouldn't have enough time to grab some paper before Andres and Hugo returned. She didn't want Andres to find out the potential business deal she had been so lucky to have made on her own.

"Do you think there is any possibility to set up the meeting online?" Melissa asked, handing the napkin to Gloria. "I don't always have the opportunity to visit London as often as I would like."

Gloria raised her eyebrows. "Sorry, I didn't make myself clear, *all* the meetings need to be online due to the company's decision-makers being in South America."

Melissa gave Gloria a hopeful smile with bright eyes. "Really?"

Gloria leaned towards her and winked. "Really."

Before Melissa could thank her for the opportunity, the door swung open and Hugo stormed into the salon.

"Gloria, pick up your things, we are leaving!" he ordered.

Melissa flinched at Hugo's sudden appearance and spilt tea on the carpet, but Gloria remained calm. "No problem at all, *cariño*," she said, grabbing her small handbag and getting to her feet.

Hugo turned to Melissa. "Good night, Melissa."

"Night, Hugo," Melissa replied in a small voice, unsure how to react to his current mood.

Melissa followed Hugo and Gloria through the entrance hall to the main door, and Gloria turned to embrace her in a tight hug.

"It has been a pleasure, Melissa," Gloria chirped into her ear.

"Likewise," Melissa replied.

Gloria pulled away and Hugo slipped her fur coat around her shoulders. The couple stepped outside when Hugo glanced back at Melissa with a furious intensity in his eyes. He examined every inch of her body until his gaze stopped at her breasts. Melissa burned with a passionate longing as her breasts swelled and grew heavy under his gaze.

Melissa remembered Hugo's strong hands around her waist in her father's kitchen, but the slam of the door forced her out of her idyllic trance. She froze in the silent hallway and exhaled to relax her tense muscles. If only she could turn back time.

After a moment to herself, she returned to the salon where the fire had died and the dishes had been cleared, leaving Melissa with no reason to hang around, but as she turned back and headed for her room, she noticed the thin gap of light from under Andres' office door.

Under normal circumstances, she would have popped in to wish her newlywed husband goodnight and maybe initiate a passionate encounter in the office, but there had been nothing normal about their relationship from the start, so Melissa darted to her room before Andres found her. But as she undressed and removed her make-up, Andres entered the room without knocking.

Melissa sighed. "Andres, I've told you a hundred times to knock before you enter, that's what I do before entering your room. It's called *common courtesy!*"

Andres ignored her plea and continued to wheel inside. He paused and eyed the fresh flowers on the windowsill, which Melissa had brought in to make herself feel less depressed in the mornings.

"I can't have fresh flowers in the house, they give me allergies," Andres informed her.

Melissa stared at him through the mirror and said, "Well, you must be glad they're in my room and not yours."

"I'm unimpressed by your smart commentary, but regardless, you need to get rid of them. If I need to enter your room, I need to move around safely."

Melissa slammed her brush on the table and swallowed her frustration, counting to ten in her mind. There was no point arguing with him. "Sure, fine, I'll get rid of them."

Andres nodded with approval and lifted a folded bra from the bed.

"I see you have changed into your sexy lingerie."

Melissa whipped her head around and launched over to him, ripping the garment from his hands. "What do you think you're doing? Give it back!"

Andres shrugged and moved to her desk. He touched one of her make-up brushes and inspected the different bottles on the table, leaving an unorganised mess on the desk.

Melissa crossed her arms and huffed. "What do you want, Andres?"

"I'm surprised you use all these things. You usually make no effort on your face most days," Andres criticised. "You looked more or less decent today, but the *Gorgeous Garcia* stole the dim spotlight from you when she arrived."

"I don't like using much make-up – not in the way you prefer, anyway," Melissa defended.

Melissa struggled with constant pangs of jealousy throughout the evening, but since Gloria made the effort to speak to her and offer her an accountancy role, she felt a little more equal. Her body still longed for Hugo's touch, and Andres' insults would always sting, but she no longer saw the point in trying to compete.

"Yes, I can tell. Thank *God* Hugo brought *Miss Leggy Garcia* to lighten the mood of the party! It got so *boring* in the dining room."

Melissa expected Andres to lash out at her for refusing to eat the veal, but to her surprise, he didn't bring it up. Instead, he crossed his arms and eyed the ceiling with a pervy grin.

"Ah, Miss. Garcia, I can't seem to get enough of her," Andres said. "That voluptuous body, full breasts and such long legs! She must be a pistol in bed."

A burning fury fired through Melissa as Andres spoke about Gloria like a piece of meat, but she resisted the urge to slap him and rolled her eyes.

"Is there something I can do for you?" she pressed.

"Oh, yes, I came here to tell you something," Andres replied, returning to reality. "I know you must have sexual urges what with being married to someone unable to satisfy your needs. Although, If you looked like Miss Garcia, the situation might be different."

"Just get to the point, Andres, will you?" Melissa pressed, tired of his games.

"… but I cannot risk you tarnishing the family name by having secret affairs. So, I have arranged for you to have sex with my brother once a month."

"Wait, *what?!*" Melissa gasped.

"It makes sense," Andres justified as if he were making a casual business deal. "Hugo looks exactly like me, and since he would have sex with a broomstick if he could, he has promised to help me out."

The intense stare Hugo had given her before he left with Gloria flickered through Melissa's mind. Had he been measuring her up to see if she met his criteria?

Melissa straightened her tense posture and said, "I don't think it will be necessary, I would rather live in celibacy for the rest of my life."

Andres grinned with amusement. "That's what all women say, but you will soon be looking for someone to satisfy your physical needs, making me look like an idiot."

Melissa shook her head in disbelief. "I can't believe I'm having this ridiculous conversation!"

"Anyway, he is coming tomorrow to take care of things," Andres continued, ignoring Melissa's disagreement. "But he has only agreed to the maximum of an hour. I don't want him to overindulge himself after *Miss*

Leggy Garcia."

A sudden thought of Gloria popped into her mind. "What about Gloria? He can't do that to her."

Andres burst into laughter. "Melissa, do you really think she cares if he is faithful to her or not? My God, you're so naive! She probably has sex with a different guy every night before sleeping next to my brother."

The idea of competing with Gloria for Hugo's attention filled her with nausea, especially after Gloria's kindness and their unexpected business deal.

"I can't do it!" Melissa protested. "You can't force me!"

Andres raised his hands in defeat. "You're right, I can't, but what I can do is call the bank tomorrow morning and request for them to sell your father's house to the company in London who are dying to rip it to pieces and build a hotel complex there."

All the blood drained from Melissa's pale face as she froze and stared at Andres.

"There would be nothing left of your precious family home, but suit yourself, you make the decision," Andres continued, wheeling away.

What decision? Melissa thought, wanting to scream, but the bitter taste of defeat invaded her mouth.

"I'll do it," she said.

Andres turned and displayed his wolf smile. "There's the girl I married."

Melissa took a deep breath. "It's only an hour, once a month?"

Andres nodded. "Correct."

"And you won't be there?" Melissa asked, blushing as the question escaped her lips.

Andres' eyes widened. "Well, I didn't know you require an audience, but I must disappoint you, darling. Any sexual activity with you would be comparable to *a dead fish* and bore my manhood quicker than you can undress."

Andres chuckled and wheeled into his bedroom, closing the door behind him.

Melissa stood rigid and stared at the closed door, her mouth agape. Her stomach gurgled with queasiness, and she worried she would vomit her dinner.

She couldn't believe the nature of the conversation and felt dirty already. Surely, Hugo wouldn't betray his girlfriend. Gloria told her that they had shared a *wow* moment when they had met. Surely, no one who experiences that wants to cheat on their partner.

After battling with the moralities in her mind, a glimpse of hope shone through when she realised that Hugo must have agreed to keep Andres quiet. Perhaps they would just spend the hour talking before Hugo went home to Gloria.

Maybe after a couple of months, Melissa would come to trust Hugo enough to reveal her hopeless situation, but for now, she turned the lights out so she could get as much sleep as possible before Andres woke her up in a couple of hours for his glass of water.

10 CHAPTER

"Why are you so quiet, *cariño?*" Gloria asked as she adjusted her short dress in the car. "I thought the night was a success in all possible ways."

"Hmm?" Hugo murmured, keeping his eyes on the road.

Hugo should have known that his brother's envy over him had no limits, but he never thought Andres' desire to continue their obsessive sibling rivalry extended to the dark levels he had revealed back at the Ferrero mansion. Andres had clearly found Hugo's weak spot and masked the situation shamelessly behind his medical condition, which had sparked the argument. Whilst Hugo's body ached for Melissa and fired with rage every time Andres called her "darling", he wouldn't dream of touching his brother's wife, no matter how much the blue-eyed witch haunted his mind.

Hugo yanked the steering wheel and Gloria gasped with fear.

"Easy, tiger, you don't want to kill us both tonight. There is still so much to live for!" Gloria cried.

"Or to die for," Hugo mumbled, slowing the speed of the car.

"I don't understand, Hugo, if you like her so much, why didn't you approach her long before she married your brother?" Gloria questioned. "Despite the mobility difference, you both look *exactly* the same, so if she fancies your brother, there wouldn't be any reason why she wouldn't like *you* as well."

Hugo smiled with cynicism.

Gloria's naïve, inaccurate conclusions often amused Hugo, but on this occasion, he appreciated the seed of truth in her words. Even though he had made a move on Melissa first, she had clearly been looking for someone vulnerable enough to fall for her greedy plans.

As Hugo continued to drive home, he reflected on the argument that caused him to storm out.

When Melissa had escaped from the dining room, he had stayed in the room to finish the black coffee Mrs Whittle had prepared for him, and Andres had wheeled into the room.

"Looks like you're not worried at all for your little girlfriend, Brother. What happened, troubles in the paradise?"

Hugo grinned. "I trust her with my life."

Andres raised an eyebrow. "Well, then it looks like your life is not worth much as she was just about to kiss me when Melissa entered the room. Jealous obviously, poor girl, but who could say no to Miss Gloria?"

"Last time I checked, you are not an animal. Therefore, why don't you just keep your dick in your pants and respect your wife for a change?" Hugo said, glugging the last of the coffee and standing up.

Andres ignored his words. "That being said, would you join me in my office for a quick whiskey and cigarette? I need to speak to you."

"What is it?" Hugo questioned.

He wished not to discuss anything with his brother, but since they still did business together, it might be something very important.

"It's delicate in nature, so I would rather discuss it behind closed doors if you don't mind?"

"Whatever," Hugo said and followed Andres.

On the way to his office, Hugo leered around to catch a glimpse of both women, but neither of them were on the scene. Maybe better that way; seeing Melissa made his blood boil.

"What is it?" Hugo asked as he closed the office door behind them both.

"Patience, my dearest brother. How many times we have had the luxury of time to enjoy each other's company like this?" Andres asked and lit a cigarette.

Hugo laughed. "We both know we haven't enjoyed each other's company since we were in nappies, so spit it out, what is it you wish to discuss with me?"

"Well, as you know since the accident my libido has been quite selective. The doctors keep telling me it will change once I recover, but as it stands, I struggle to…" He paused to find the words. "…to finish the job with my wife."

Hugo's heart rate quickened. He wished nothing but happiness for his brother, but the idea of Andres and Melissa living a platonic relationship gave him a new type of hope he didn't recognise until Andres's next words shattered his world.

"It's not like we haven't done things. On the contrary, she is very eager to satisfy my needs in all creative ways, if you know what I mean, but I would like to return a favour from my end."

Hugo's expression darkened. "Are you done bragging about your sex life with your wife?"

Andres ignored his words. "Anyhow, I was thinking… since I'm still recovering, and we both look alike… you wouldn't mind finishing the job for me until I'm fully recovered?"

"Finish what job?"

"Have sex with her on a regular basis."

"What?! Are you insane?"

"Actually, if you think about it, it's brilliant! I get to recover, and I wouldn't have to worry about her looking for another man's company."

Hugo was still processing his brother's request when his words hit him. "What do you mean another man's company?"

"Well, I wish not to brag with what I'm about to tell you, but she has given me an ultimatum to satisfy her needs, or she will look around for someone else who can do it for her, and frankly, I can't blame her," Andres said, burying his head in his palms.

Hugo approached his brother and tapped his back. "Look, man, I had no idea. I don't know what to say."

That bitch.

Despite their difficult relationship, Hugo pitied Andres.

"It's ok. I knew she only married me for money anyway so this is something I should have expected. Tell me you will take care of it until I feel better? I don't want people to laugh at me behind my back. I have enough to adjust in life with this stupid chair!"

Hugo's eyes narrowed. "What do you mean she married you only for money?"

"I don't know, something about her father's house she couldn't afford to buy it. That's what she has been telling me since the wedding."

Hugo grew quiet, processing the information. Despite the new information he had learnt about Melissa, the idea of having her underneath him at his mercy made his jeans tighten. But even if Hugo wanted to help his brother, he was afraid that touching Melissa would open the can of worms he wasn't prepared for. How could he stop once he started?

"I don't know, man. That's sick. Besides, I have Gloria in my life. I wouldn't want to disappoint her in any way."

"Well, I'm not going to beg. I'll ask someone else from the city, then. I'm sure they don't mind. Even if she is not my cup of tea, she is not the worst sight for sore eyes."

"No!" Jealousy twisted in Hugo's stomach.

It was difficult enough to imagine *his brother* touching her, but he would be *damned* to let anyone else touch her.

Andres's mouth quivered into a smile. "I knew I could trust you, Brother. One hour, once a month. Make it quick. I swear Gloria won't find out from me."

On some level, Hugo understood Melissa's desire to buy his father's house, even if she had married his brother for money, but that didn't explain why she would want to flaunt her sexuality and threaten to engage in promiscuous affairs just to ridicule his brother. After all, his brother had saved her.

"Why don't you just tell her to wait? Women wait all the time to find a boyfriend or husband without engaging in one-night stands."

Andres' head jerked back, and he laughed. "My god, you are so naive, Brother! Where have you lived in the past decade? Besides, have you seen her mother? She has probably more feathers in her hat than there are men in Canford Cliffs!"

Hugo couldn't deny the rumours Melissa's mum had inflicted in town when she had divorced Melissa's dad and considering how generously Melissa had offered herself to Hugo the day in her kitchen, who knew what Melissa was capable of… after all, she was a product of both her parents.

"Well, I don't have all night for this. Are you in or out?"

Without weighing his response further, Hugo stood up from the sofa and stormed out. "I'll do it!"

Stupid bitch won't know what hit her, Hugo thought, returning from his recollection of the argument.

"Are you ok, *mi vida*? You look preoccupied like a psycho," Gloria jested.

"You are quite right, my dear, you are quite right," Hugo replied, adjusting his posture in his seat.

He couldn't wait to be back in a short twelve hours.

11 CHAPTER

The night turned into morning too soon and Melissa woke with an icky stomach. She had spent the entire night dwelling over the next twenty-four-hours and how she could convince Hugo against obeying Andres' request. Despite the kiss they had shared in her father's house, she couldn't imagine that Hugo would *actually* cheat on Gloria, but she couldn't be sure anymore.

As Melissa enjoyed the temporary peace in her bedroom, she thought about how to tell Hugo why she had married Andres, but she dreaded his reaction and possible hatred towards her.

She still stood behind her choice of marrying Andres to save her family home, even if she knew it would make her look like a gold digger to the outside world, but the pain of losing something so dear to her weighed more than people's opinion of her. Although, she wasn't sure whether Hugo would see things from her perspective. After all, he was Andres' brother and the guilt of his accident laid heavy on his shoulders.

She glanced at the silver clock on her nightstand and her heart plummeted.

"Shit!" she exclaimed, jumping out of bed.

It was only 8.30 am but she had her weekly meeting with her boss in less than five minutes. Without the time to shower, Melissa powered up her computer and brushed her golden locks into a tight ponytail. She changed into a pair of black leather trousers and a sky-blue cardigan, not forgetting to wash her face and apply some natural makeup too.

After getting comfortable on her desk chair, she took a deep breath and joined the online meeting. Having worn her high heels all last night, she slipped into leather slides that had a comfortable furry coating inside. She exhaled deeply and closed her eyes as she felt her tired feet resting against the soft cushion of the slides.

"Melissa, I have been waiting for you all morning!" her boss said.

Melissa smiled with apology and said, "Good morning to you too, Jason."

Jason ignored her greeting and paced his office on the screen. Melissa frowned and tilted her head.

"Jason, what's wrong?"

"Nothing's wrong, Melissa, we've just had the biggest breakthrough in company history!"

"Oh," Melissa replied, her mood sinking. "Someone has landed a big deal in the office?"

"You bet someone has!" Jason yelled, running his fingers excitedly on the keyboard.

"Well, I'm happy for them. New business is always good, and I know organic growth is an important element, especially for partners like yourself, Jason."

Even though she felt happy, she couldn't resist feeling slight envy in her heart. There had been a time when *she* had been the one bringing new business to the company. In fact, she had been rewarded for it many years in a row and rumour had it that she had been making her way to the next associate.

How life could make a U-turn in a blink of an eye, she thought.

"Oh? That's all you can say?" Jason exclaimed, eying her through the screen.

Melissa shrugged. "Well, I believe congratulations are in order?"

Jason scoffed with amusement. "My God, Melissa, don't be so modest and tell me how you did it!"

Melissa's heart rate tripled, and her hands clammed with sweat. "What do you mean, Jason?"

"Jeez, Melissa you're thick this morning! Did you party all night or did Miss. Garcia make you work to earn your reputation?"

Melissa's eyes widened and Jason nodded. "Do I have your attention now or do you know all the details already?"

She shook her head. "Don't tell me Gloria called the office this morning?"

Jason grinned. "Happy to see you're on a first name basis with her, but no, Miss. Garcia didn't call – her lawyers did!"

"Get out!" Melissa shouted with excitement as her lips quivered into a smile. "What did they say?!"

"I certainly won't, darling, and after this, you won't get rid of me ever!" Jason smirked.

He cleared his throat and explained the details; Melissa learnt that Gloria was not only a partner but also *the chairman* of Garcia Industries. The company made sure to eliminate corruption, and they improved their contractual position to ensure that the small business owners were compensated fairly for their hard work. They also had small offices in exotic locations, such as Guatemala and Argentina, where Gloria had spent most of her time over the last year without anyone seeing her.

That's where she must have met Hugo, Melissa thought, and her mind wandered to the conversation she had with Andres last night and the events yet to come.

A shot of guilt stabbed her in the heart as she recognised that Gloria had seen potential in her and given her company an amazing opportunity.

"– and they want *you* to deliver it!" Jason finished.

Melissa blinked. "I'm sorry, Jason, what did you say?"

"Melissa, focus please, this is important," Jason said, narrowing his eyes for the first time. "Are you ok?"

"Of course, I just didn't sleep well, that's all," Melissa replied through a loud yawn.

Jason chuckled. "And here I thought the sea air made everyone sleep like a baby."

Melissa laughed. "You would be surprised."

"Trust me, love, I have no intention of leaving London, but you should definitely consider coming back to visit us at least," Jason said before he returned to his notes.

Melissa listened tentatively and made notes about how to get things started with Garcia Industries, but the more Jason spoke, the more she realised how much she missed London. She sighed and wondered whether she could get Hugo to convince Andres to let her go back for a few days.

***

A few hours later, the meeting ended and Melissa closed her notebook full of tasks.
It would take a great deal of her time to finish the investigation into Garcia Industries and gain access to their accounts, but she didn't mind using her endless time to work. After all, she would do anything to take her mind away from the mansion and all within.

Melissa took a few moments to herself before she headed downstairs to grab breakfast.

She sighed with relief as she entered the empty kitchen, and her spirits had lifted due to her new responsibility, but as she hummed around the kitchen and prepared her Mediterranean breakfast, a familiar voice startled her.

"Penny for your thoughts."

Melissa shrieked as one of the pots slipped from her hand and crashed onto the floor. She turned to see Hugo smirking in the doorway.

"What are you doing here?" she asked, grabbing the pot from the floor.

"We need to stop meeting like this," Hugo said, repeating Melissa's words the day he appeared in her father's kitchen.

"If it was down to me, we wouldn't be meeting at all," Melissa replied.

Hugo ignored her sharp comment and thoughtfully eyed her petite frame. "Mm, you're much shorter than I remember."

Melissa wanted to remind him that she usually wore high heels, but Hugo's intense stare created goosebumps on her skin and tingles in places she didn't want to think about in his presence.

"Blame it on my parents," Melissa said, challenging him with her stare.

Hugo broke eye contact and changed the subject. "I believe you spoke to your husband?"

Melissa froze. *It was now or never.* "I did."

"I take it you pushed for the idea?" Hugo quipped.

Melissa jerked her head up. "Excuse me?"

Hugo's features hardened. "You told him you were bored and considered an affair to hurt him for not being able to satisfy your needs?

The needs you perfectly knew he could not fulfil before you married him!"

Melissa scoffed. "You're insane."

"Am I?" Hugo asked, prowling towards her like a panther.

Melissa's eyes followed his movements. "I would never say such things to anyone."

"Sometimes, it's not the things you say but the actions you take, just like animals."

Melissa frowned. "Did you just compare me to an animal?"

Hugo froze and scowled. "Considering your behaviour and how you're treating my brother – yes."

"I've treated your brother with nothing but respect!" Melissa cried, stepping away from Hugo.

"Is that so?" Hugo questioned, trapping Melissa in the corner of the kitchen.

Hugo's masculine scent gave Melissa butterflies, but she swallowed hard and remained blank.

"I give you credit for thinking you can fool my brother - he has always been simple in some ways, but you're damn wrong if you think you can fool me or ridicule my family!" Hugo warned. "I *always* look after my family."

"I never wanted to be part of your family."

"Yet, you sneaked into it by using my brother's weakest moment?"

"Yet, *you* created his weak moment," Melissa quipped.

Hugo flared his nostrils and huffed with agitation. Melissa expected a smack, but Hugo continued to glower at her instead.

She regretted them immediately. Unlike the Ferrero family, she didn't enjoy hurting people.

"Look, we're both heated and clearly have different opinions, so I think it would be better to have a cup of tea and talk," Melissa suggested.

She turned to get two cups from the shelf, but Hugo had other ideas. He grabbed Melissa's shoulder and wrenched her around, making her jump with alarm.

Melissa feared an attack, but Hugo brought his face close to hers and stared at her lips, giving Melissa the intoxicating urge to bridge the gap between them.

"I will do whatever my brother asks me to do because I *owe* it to him, but make no mistakes, I have no empathy for someone as manipulative as you, and I'll make sure you don't embarrass my family."

"How dare you—"

"And you can tell your boss to stop calling you *love* or *darling*, that's my brother's privilege."

Melissa gasped and pushed him away. "You *eavesdropped* on my work conversation?"

His chest was hard and muscular, and Melissa could feel his lungs filling with air as he took a surprised step back, gripping her wrists. "It's my responsibility to look after my brother, so I need to ensure that you won't embarrass him with any secret *escapades* with your boss, on screen or in person."

Melissa already knew what was yet to come as she heard her voice come out as a quiet whimper.

"In person?" Melissa questioned.

Hugo raised his thick eyebrows and mockingly caressed her arms with his fingertips. "If I didn't make myself clear, you won't be visiting London anytime soon."

Melissa's hope melted away like sugar in the rain.

"You can't be serious! I have work to do!" Melissa panicked, her eyes welling with tears.

"You should have thought about that before flirting with your boss."

Melissa ripped her arms free and glared at him. "You can't tell me what to do, it's the 21st century for crying out loud!"

Hugo grabbed her waist and jerked her towards him. Melissa gasped and tried to avoid leaning against him, but his strength made her resistance impossible.

"If I were you, I would play nice and wait until the evening. I'm sure you will find a way to convince me to take you to London with my brother," Hugo challenged, staring at her lips again.

"What should I do?" Melissa cried.

"You'll find a way," Hugo whispered.

Melissa gazed into Hugo's eyes, and he leaned in to kiss her. Melissa pulled her head away, but Hugo leaned in farther so she couldn't escape. His tongue found its way into her mouth and Melissa soon melted into the moment.

Her body relaxed with pleasure and the feel of his tongue heated her abdomen, making her desperate to rub herself against him. She swirled her tongue around Hugo's mouth when he tore himself away and shoved Melissa backwards. She smacked her lower back on the handrail of the hob and winced with pain.

"I should have known - my brother was right! You're a disgrace to our family name and he should never have married you!" Hugo roared. "I wish I had been here to tell him that!"

Melissa recovered with haste and forced back the tears. "Then don't come back here before I'm gone!"

Hugo turned and stormed towards the door. "Trust me, you will be here to pay back every single penny. I will make sure of it. At least once a month."

For a second, Melissa thought Andres stood before her.

"You can't be serious," she whispered, biting her lip.

Like a panther that had enjoyed its first kill, Hugo licked his lips and ogled at Melissa. "You have seven hours until I come back, so make the most of it."

A moment later, Hugo left the kitchen and stormed out the front door.

Melissa buried her face in her palms and sobbed on the kitchen counter. Her hope to get Hugo onside had been destroyed, and Melissa felt like a bird trapped in a locked cage.

Melissa rubbed her lips on her sleeve, but his touch continued to burn into her skin. She poured a cup of tea to calm her nerves, but she didn't fancy her Mediterranean brunch anymore.

***

After the incident with Hugo in the kitchen, Melissa washed up her teacup and hurried back to her room to change into her outdoor gear, but on the way outside, she ran into Andres in the hallway.

"Where have you been? I've been looking all over you!" Andres complained.

"I'm sorry, Andres, I had my weekly meeting with my boss and then I had tea and crackers in the kitchen."

Andres huffed. "I don't understand why the guy keeps you on his payroll, it's not like you work with him anymore."

Melissa shrugged and ignored his wittering, but Andres noticed and continued to dig further.

"From a business perspective, you should allow him to recruit someone else to replace you. Someone who is actually *useful* for them and able to *commit* to deadlines," he said with a smug smile.

Melissa had never told Andres the details of her work, so she felt no shame in keeping the morning's good news to herself.

"You're quite right, Andres, he is a kind man," she agreed, heading to the door.

"Where are you going?" Andres demanded.

Melissa stopped at the door. "For a quick run at the beach. Do you want to come with me? I'm sure I can find a way to the beach with the wheelchair. We could both use a breath of fresh air."

Andres scoffed. "How dare you mock my condition like this!"

Melissa rolled her eyes at Andres' narcissism and turned back to the door.

"I'll be back in a couple of hours. I'm sure Mrs Whittle will take care of your needs until then," she said.

"I would think so since you've never been good at caring for my needs anyway," Andres complained as Melissa grabbed the door handle. "Oh, and make sure you stay within Ferrero Estates. You know the deal if you try to disappear."

Melissa shivered as the cold air hit her skin, but after walking to the back of the mansion and down the old stone steps that led to the Ferrero beachside, she felt a little warmer.

As Melissa ambled onto the beach, she enjoyed the wind and the sound of the waves crashing against the sand. She perched herself down and made the most of her time alone.

"Dad, I wish you were here to guide me," she whispered into the air as a lonely tear trickled down her cold cheek. "I know you wouldn't be proud of me for what I've done, but I had no choice. I couldn't lose my only memory of you."

As Melissa stared out to sea, a loud crack sounded in the bushes behind her. She sprung to her feet and turned around.

"Who is there?" she shouted.

Melissa remembered that foxes and other animals inhabited the forestry near the beach, but she feared something, or someone, bigger.

"Hello!" she yelled, grabbing a wet stick from the sand.

Melissa had never been a wildlife expert, but she knew most wild animals feared sudden sounds, so she whacked the stick onto a nearby rock to create some noise.

She watched the forest behind her for a couple of minutes, but after nothing else suspicious happened, she calmed down. Melissa glanced at her watch and sighed. She had a few hours left before dinner time.

12 CHAPTER

Before dinner, Melissa decided to indulge herself in a proper spa treatment with one of the big, expensive bath bombs Mrs Whittle had ordered from *Lush* online.

Screw them!

She bathed until her skin softened and naturally smelled like vanilla and jasmine and dried herself with a fluffy towel. She changed into a pink balconette bra with matching knickers and dressed in a white pencil skirt and silk blouse.

Melissa critically eyed her reflection in the mirror. She didn't want to come across that she was expecting the night but didn't want to give the impression of being scared either. Her outfit would have been suitable for an office environment, which contrasted with Gloria's choice of style, but Melissa refused to change her style just to compete with her.

She took a seat at her desk and got started with her hair and makeup. For her own sake, Melissa didn't want to step over the line and raise suspicion, so she applied a simple smokey eye and her Charlotte Tilbury lipstick, and instead of blush, she lightly pinched her cheeks to increase the blood circulation, giving her a healthy glow. Melissa left her hair to air-dry for as long as possible and blow-dried her ends into soft curls.

Melissa admired herself in the mirror when the front door opened, and Mrs Whittle's loud voice echoed upstairs.

"Good evening, Mr Ferrero, I'm pleasantly surprised to see that you've arrived on time, it's definitely a first," Melissa heard her say.

Melissa's heart pounded as she heard the familiar voices downstairs. She sprayed some perfume behind her ears and on her wrists and slipped into a pair of nude heels. She exhaled and made her way downstairs, but when she spotted Hugo at the main entrance, she lost her footing and stumbled.

Hugo gasped and charged over to Melissa, saving her from plummeting to the floor.

"Melissa, are you ok?" he asked with alarm.

Melissa paused with surprise and met Hugo's gaze. His dark eyes reflected genuine concern and something else Melissa couldn't quite put her finger on.

"I'm perfectly fine," Melissa assured, regaining her balance.

Hugo let her go immediately but kept his hands ready to catch her again. "You shouldn't wear those heels all the time. Why don't you wear something more comfortable?"

Melissa shook her head. "It's not the heels. I haven't eaten anything since this morning, so I feel a little lightheaded, that's all."

Hugo frowned. "You should take better care of yourself; the magic of the fresh sea air doesn't work if you don't eat."

Hugo offered his hand to escort her to the dining room, but Melissa paused and realised what he had meant.

"You followed me to the beach?!" she hissed, taking his arm.

"I wouldn't say *followed;* I was in the neighbourhood," Hugo replied in a casual tone.

"The same *bloody* thing!" Melissa snapped. "Why don't you just leave me alone?"

Melissa tore her hand from Hugo's arm and they both entered the dining room.

"About time! I've been waiting for twenty-minutes at least!" Andres sulked as Melissa sat next to him.

"Apologies, Brother. I thought the invitation was for 8.30 pm, which would make me exactly on time."

Melissa smirked at Hugo's defence and admired his courage to stand up for himself.

For the first time, Andres didn't respond in his usual poisonous manner. Instead, he sipped his red wine and stayed silent.

Melissa placed her hand on his shoulder and dipped her brow. "Andres, are you feeling well?"

Andres pushed her hand away and scowled. "I feel fine, I'm just annoyed that you always make me wait and feel bad about myself."

Melissa swallowed her response and said nothing. Andres would only yell if she replied.

A few moments later, the waitress served the mushroom soup as an appetizer and Melissa smiled as a thank you.

The three of them kept up light conversation and Melissa avoided eye contact with Hugo throughout the meal, but his tight jeans and white dress shirt made her tingle. She noticed that he had left a couple of the top buttons undone, offering her a sneak peek of his muscular body covered in soft dark hair. For a second, Melissa imagined herself running her hand through his soft curls and caressing his hard body. Had he done it on purpose?

"So, Brother, where is your lovely bride-to-be tonight?"

Melissa's hand froze in the air as she waited for Hugo's response.

"Actually, Brother, she had to travel overseas to attend to business matters, but don't worry, she will be back soon enough."

Andres' face fell. "When did she leave?"

Hugo chewed a piece of meat and swallowed before he continued. "I dropped her off at the airport on my way here."

"Oh, in that case, you must be exhausted after spending all day with Miss. Garcia," Andres replied, grinning at Melissa knowingly.

Melissa clenched her jaw at the thought of Hugo and Gloria in a passionate embrace, but she sipped her drink to hide her sorrow.

"Something like that," Hugo confirmed, filling Melissa with dread.

After dinner, Andres retreated to his office with Hugo and Melissa returned to her room. She glanced between the clock to the beach view out the window and twisted her wedding ring with anxiety. Perhaps she should just forget her father's house and escape through the forest – then she could return to London and forget the last few weeks.

"Looking for ways to escape?" Hugo questioned as he entered the room.

Melissa jumped and huffed with frustration. "Didn't your mother ever teach you both to *knock* before entering someone else's room?"

"Well, considering my family *paid* for all this and I continue to pay for it, I have the right to enter any room I like."

Melissa straightened her posture. "*This* room has been assigned to me since I moved in, and as the new *Mrs Ferrero*, I have the right to demand respect in it."

Melissa shuffled her feet with embarrassment and cleared her throat. She instantly regretted parading her new title, but she was too stubborn to take it back.

Hugo raised an eyebrow and lifted his hands in surrender. "My apologies, *Mrs Ferrero*. May I come in?"

Melissa hesitated and savoured her minor victory, but she nodded, and Hugo stepped inside. He locked the door behind him and turned back to Melissa. The lock on the door sounded like a bullet leaving a gun.

"So, how do you want to do this?" he asked in a casual tone.

"Andres didn't give you specific instructions?" Melissa mocked.

"Well, actually no, he just told me to *fuck you* the way I like and try to keep my dick hard after my afternoon with Gloria."

Hugo's words wounded Melissa's soul, but she kept a blank expression to hide her pain.

"Well, in that case, why don't we just pretend to…" her voice trailed off. "…to do stuff?"

Hugo laughed. "As much as I would like to pretend anything with you, *Lizzy*, pretending wouldn't erase my brother's concern of you cheating on him and disrespecting the whole family."

He had called her Lizzy. Her father's pet name he had once given her a long time ago.

Melissa scoffed. "Come on, Hugo. You can't seriously suggest that we hop in the sack just to make sure I won't cheat on your brother! What kind of person do you think I am?"

"All I can see is a woman who saw a wealthy man on his knees, trying to get used to his new life in a wheelchair, desperate for affection and warmth," Hugo spat. "Just like your mother, full of greed. If she didn't drive your father into financial despair, he'd still be alive."

"How dare you suggest that my father died because of my mother!" Melissa hissed.

Hugo shrugged and unbuttoned his white shirt. "Maybe not purposefully, but that doesn't mean it didn't happen. People do many things unintentionally with crucial consequences."

The meaning of his last words was left unnoticed as Melissa stared at his hands with wide eyes. "What are you doing?"

Hugo sniggered. "As much as this conversation excites me, I have an early meeting tomorrow and I would like to take care of this as quickly as possible and make my way."

"All the more reason for not doing it and plotting how to convince your brother that we have."

Hugo's hand stopped on the zipper of his black jeans.

"Are you seriously suggesting that we *plot* our way out of this?" Hugo questioned, but Melissa didn't respond. "I don't know why you thought I would be on your side. *I hate you*, Melissa, but I will always look after my family no matter what happens."

"How can you say that? You don't even know me!" Melissa cried.

"I don't care to know you after what I've discovered so far. I'm only here to do what my brother requested," Hugo said. "Now, are you going to undress, or shall I do it for you?"

"You can't seriously suggest that we do this?" Melissa exclaimed, biting her lip. "What about Gloria? I thought you loved her!"

Hugo approached Melissa in just his black jeans, and she ogled his sun-kissed chest and abs. She could clearly see his body was built outdoors instead of in the gym. Involuntarily, she felt her body react to the sight before her as the heat built up in her joints, and the nerve centre between her legs tingled.

"Leave Gloria out of this," Hugo ordered.

With a shirtless body and jeans that barely sat on his hips, Hugo looked more dangerous than ever, and *handsome*, but Melissa stepped away.

"Don't come closer to me! This is wrong, and illegal in this country. You can't force me to sleep with you!"

"Maybe not," Hugo agreed, stopping and shoving his hands in his pockets. "But in that case, I will ensure that my brother sells your father's house to Cheap Holidays first thing tomorrow morning."

Melissa furrowed her brow. "How do you know about that?"

Melissa's voice broke down. She felt defeated.

"I know all sorts of things that are important to the business," Hugo replied, bridging the gap between them and grabbing her waist.

"Is that what I am to you, a business?" Melissa whispered against his chest.

Although Hugo had forced himself against Melissa, she felt at peace against his warm body as the weight of the world lifted from her shoulders.

Hugo lifted her chin and stared into her teary eyes.

"I don't want to hurt you, and if all goes as planned, you might even enjoy it. I know I may not be your first choice, but I'm not the ugliest *cabrón* in the block either."

A childlike question escaped from Melissa's lips. "What is cabrón?"

Hugo smiled. "A bastard."

"Why can't you just let me go?" Melissa whispered as Hugo kissed her cheek.

"I have my reasons."

Melissa turned her head to question his reasons, but Hugo pressed his lips onto hers and pushed his tongue into her mouth. Melissa closed her eyes and massaged his thick, black hair with her fingers.

Hugo took her response as an invitation and trailed his hand towards the only button on her silk blouse.

"Can I open it?" Hugo murmured against her lips.

"I'd rather you didn't," Melissa whispered, but her words lacked authority.

Hugo smiled and unbuttoned her shirt anyway. "Oops."

Despite the situation, Melissa grinned. "You are impossible."

Hugo smiled. "I'll take that as a compliment."

As Hugo planted small kisses along her neckline, Melissa could feel her body respond to his touch, but the sight of her wedding ring reminded her of Andres.

"No, I can't do this," she exclaimed, pushing Hugo away. "I'm sorry, I will do whatever you want me to do, just not this. I don't feel well, I think I'm sick."

Melissa hurried to the door when Hugo seized her waist and forced her around. Melissa writhed in his grip and managed to bite his arm, but Hugo pushed her onto the bed and leapt on top of her.

"Do you think this is a big deal? You're not a virgin! For all I know, you've been sleeping with different men every night, and from the way you've been flirting with your boss, the things we are about to do shouldn't come as a surprise, *Lizzy*!"

"Stop calling me *Lizzy*, you don't have the right!" she barked, struggling to free herself.

"Why not? I like the intimate sound of it. It can be our little secret now your old man is gone," Hugo pressed, ignoring her efforts to escape.

Hugo snuggled his face into her neckline and let his hands wander up her blouse until they reached her breasts. Melissa tried to force his hand away, but when he moved her bra cup aside to pinch her hardened nipple, she moaned with pleasure.

Hugo grinned and switched places with her, allowing him to remove her silk blouse and open her bra.

"Hugo, please stop," Melissa whispered.

Hugo ignored her plea and increased his pace. He opened the hidden zipper on her pencil skirt and slid down the soft fabric, only to find her nude stay-ups and matching lingerie set.

"You planned this all along!" Hugo accused, but his words lacked meaning as his appreciative gaze burned through Melissa's body, making her feel hot and beautiful for the first time in years.

Hugo leapt to his feet and removed his jeans and boxers, revealing his nakedness in its full glory.

He had been right, Melissa wasn't a virgin, but she certainly lacked experience with men as her eyes widened at the sight before her.

"That *thing* won't fit in me!" Melissa blurted, wide-eyed at his throbbing manhood.

Hugo smirked at her natural reaction and slid her knickers down her legs. "I'm sure it will, *amor mio*. Trust me."

He placed himself between her legs and caressed her swollen entrance with his gentle touch. Melissa's body jerked on the bed and Hugo's gaze intensified as he desperately waited for her sweet release.

"Any last words, my *Lizzy*?" he whispered, working his fingers inside her soft folds.

"Let it be fast and passionless," Melissa panted, but her eyes glistened with passion and anticipation.

Hugo smiled and adjusted himself between her legs. "I must apologise for disappointing you in advance then."

Hugo slid inside her, and Melissa gasped with a mixture of pain and pleasure. He paused to let her adjust to his size, but when their eyes met, he filled her and she became his in all possible ways.

13 CHAPTER

Melissa woke to the morning sunlight and realised that she had slept fully naked.

She covered her body with the white duvet and noticed that she ached in unfamiliar places, reminding her of the previous night's events with Hugo. Melissa blushed and buried her face into her palms, especially as she recalled her eagerness to please him more than once.

Not exactly as she had planned.

Hugo had been very skilful and taught her things she never knew existed and willingly she had followed him until a groundbreaking orgasm surged through her body. At the same time, Hugo had reached his climax, roaring loud like an animal. Her toes still curled out of pleasure remembering the intimate way he had touched her and found her points of pleasure in such an effortless manner, anyone would have thought *they* were married, but Melissa's mind darkened as she remembered that Hugo had chosen Gloria, and more importantly, she had chosen Andres.

The mixture of jealousy and guilt made it difficult to drag herself to the shower, but she needed to rid herself of Hugo's scent.

Melissa scrubbed her skin until it turned red and changed into her sweats. She stared at her make-up bottles and tubes, but she sighed with exhaustion.

She knew Andres wouldn't approve of her casual attire and bare face, but she didn't have the strength to do anything after the night she'd had. Melissa hoped Andres would still be asleep, but hoping didn't get her very far when she headed downstairs.

"Oh, there she is, my lovely wife in her inappropriate sweats," Andres mocked at the dining table. "I assume the night was more or less a fiasco given the scowl my brother wore when he raced out of here only an hour after arriving last night."

Andres opened the Financial Times and Melissa poured herself a glass of orange juice.

"It was ok," Melissa said, sipping her drink and helping herself to a freshly made croissant.

Andres closed the newspaper and folded it in front of him. "I take it my older brother was not able to consummate the deal after all the goodbye sex with *Leggy Garcia*."

Melissa slammed her glass onto the table and huffed. "Would you stop calling her that? Her name is Gloria! *Miss. Garcia,* if you prefer."

"Oh, I didn't know the sex was *that bad!*" Andres replied with a grin. "If I had known that Miss. Gorgeous Garcia had planned to travel, I would have scheduled my brother in for another day."

Andres filled his mouth with grapes and Melissa rolled her eyes.

"Don't worry, next time I'll make sure my brother can finish the job properly," Andres continued with a wink.

"Next time? You've got to be joking!"

The memory of the night still burned her loins, but she couldn't deal with the emotional turmoil it caused in her mind. It was simply wrong on so many levels, she lost count.

Andres shook his head. "I think this is the best arrangement ever.

One, I don't have to worry about you having affair and embarrassing me, and two, my brother can slowly and painfully make things up to me."

Melissa frowned. "How is Hugo sleeping with me painful for him or him making things up to you?"

Andres scoffed and widened his eyes. "Have you looked in the mirror? I hate to break it to you, but the moment he leaves Miss. Garcia to come and satisfy you, I think we both know to whom it's painful."

Ignoring the sting of his words, Melissa cut open the croissant and carefully spread raspberry jam between.

"So, you think your brother is hurt when he has to cheat on Gloria?" Melissa questioned.

Melissa didn't particularly want to continue the unconformable conversation as the events that happened in the bedroom should be kept private, but Hugo didn't act like he had been forced to sleep with her. After all, Melissa had quite openly offered him the option to *pretend* instead, but Hugo had refused. On the contrary, they both appeared to want more, but Hugo had been limited to an hour, so he had kissed her forehead goodnight before she drifted to sleep fully satisfied.

"My brother is not an animal, and I recognise a man in love. Hell, I used to be like him before I got stuck with you."

Melissa narrowed her eyes and suddenly wanted to know the reason for his mean behaviour.

"You were in love before your accident?" she asked.

Melissa expected him to give her a sad story about a woman who had turned her back on him after he had lost his mobility; a rational reason for his sulky attitude, but her open mind narrowed as he glared at her over the newspaper.

"I was in love with them *all*. It was the best time of my life," Andres said.

Melissa's spirit sank. "So, why don't you cut ties with Hugo if you hate him so much?"

Andres threw the newspaper across the room and slammed his hand on the table. "Because he has to pay for what he has done to me! He has always been better than me being a couple of minutes older *and* our mother's favourite, but he needs to be proven wrong!"

Melissa sighed under her breath and avoided Andres' intense stare.

"Excuse me," she said, standing from the table and leaving the room.

***

"Earth to Hugo!" Gloria said.

Hugo shook his head and looked up at the twelve men in suits around the boardroom table. They eyed him expectantly.

"In or out?" Gloria pressed.

Hugo cleared his throat and nodded. "That sounds like a deal to me."

Everyone exhaled as if they had held their breath in suspense, and they closed their leather briefcases. Hugo thanked them and sent them off before returning to his seat.

It was one of the most expensive, yet prestigious spots in London to rent out an office space, yet Hugo's father had rented not only one office space but two entire floors just for the company's headquarters, which now sat side by side with international banks and consultancy offices.

Rumour had it that once upon a time when the area had still been considered practically worthless, he had bought the land rights where the buildings now stood proud and tall, and even though he didn't technically own the buildings, he owned the land they were built on and due to uncontrolled rent regulations for commercial buildings, Hugo's family made a fortune just collecting the ground rent and leaseholds every year.

It had been a smart business and just one addition to his family's property portfolio, one of the many businesses his family was into.

Hugo glanced at the golden logo on one of the briefcases that represented Ferrero Industries, and it reminded him of Melissa's golden hair that had tickled his nose late last night as they both reached a groundbreaking climax.

He forced his wandering thoughts aside and focused on Gloria, who tapped her red fingernails against her leather folder.

"Hugo, I'm only going to say this once, you need to pick up the game. I've saved your ass for now, but the international investors are not stupid and will catch on if you're not careful. We need this deal."

"I don't need any deal," Hugo snapped. "Hell, if I didn't like my job so much, I could live without working. Better yet, the grandchildren of my grandchildren could do the same!"

As the words escaped his lips, the face of a young child with his charcoal eyes and Melissa's golden hair appeared in his mind, but he couldn't think of children, especially now.

Gloria exhaled as if to calm herself before she spoke.

"Hugo, I know neither of us really need this deal, but it's important to me and Garcia Industries. If I can save even *one* family business from the predator companies who only want to exploit them, that's all I need."

Hugo's eyes softened as he watched her. "I know, I'm sorry to take my frustration out on you."

"Well, do something about it then. Go to the gym, eat chocolate, or indulge in carnal sins, just please don't disappoint me again," Gloria said, and she sauntered out of the boardroom without turning back.

Hugo knew she was pissed. The business was a crucial part of her life, and more importantly, she wanted to show her family that *she* was important too. Yet, Hugo had nearly disappointed her in the cruellest manner.

Hugo slammed his balled fist against the table and buried his face into his palms. He wanted to do his job well, but a familiar aroma filled his nostrils as he rubbed his face. No matter how much he had scrubbed in the shower that morning, he could still smell her sweet vanilla scent on his palms.

Hugo thought he had judged Melissa unfairly. Due to her hesitation, he believed that she genuinely felt wrong for sleeping with him because of Gloria and Andres, but Melissa melting into him had debunked his judgment.

Hugo frowned, and his mind darkened as he pictured Melissa enticing another man in the same way, but he shook the thought from his head and strolled to the window. He admired the London skyline and relaxed his clenched fists.

He needed to make sure Melissa never tried to attract another man…for his brother's sake, of course.

14 CHAPTER

Over the next couple of days, Melissa buried herself into her work and tried to gain as much information about Garcia Industries as possible. Her internet connection used to be faster in London, and she lacked the office supplies that would have made her work more efficient, but she didn't mind sacrificing the hours needed to complete the work. Even her boss was content and sent out several progress reviews during the week, which Melissa gladly accepted.

He hadn't called her *darling* or *honey* since Hugo had accused Melissa of flirting with him, which filled her with relief, but she still didn't understand how Hugo knew the details of their work conversation.

Speaking of Hugo, Melissa hadn't heard from him since their first *session*. It's not that she *wanted* to sleep with him again and oppose her morals, but she couldn't deny the sexual tension that had been between them since the kiss they shared in her father's house. Melissa also couldn't deny her satisfaction with Hugo's skillful hands, which made her forget everything that troubled her.

To make matters worse, Gloria had taken Melissa under her wing and emailed her on regular basis to make sure she had everything she needed. In any other circumstance, Melissa would have been flattered and excited about the business relationship they shared, but the betrayal bubbling underneath the surface made her stomach twinge with nausea every time she saw a new message from her.

But a week later, an email from Hugo waited in her inbox:

Good morning, Lizzy, I hope you have recovered from our meet-up last month. The next one will be in less than two weeks, so I wanted to know if there is anything specific you would like to see. Hugo

Hugo's email made Melissa's stomach twist with butterflies, and she forgot about the task at hand.

She had asked him never to use her father's pet name for her, but reading it on the screen only reminded her of the moment when he shouted it as he had climaxed, making her body ache for him even more. But Melissa couldn't express her deep desire for him, so she opened her online calendar with the hope that Hugo had been joking in his email.

Melissa leaned away from the screen as she realised that Hugo had been correct, and she deleted his message.

She returned to her task, full of determination, when another email popped into her inbox:

Lizzy, I can see you're online, so you better respond to me. Deleting my emails won't make them less real. How are you? Hugo

Melissa gaped and scratched her head with amazement as she reread Hugo's accurate guess and eyed the computer with suspicion. Her heart rate increased at the idea of him secretly watching her through the webcam, and she played with the idea of removing her cardigan to give him a better look at her delicate figure. But she quickly realised the insanity of her thoughts and blushed as she deleted his second email.

She closed the laptop and decided to take the day off so she could read and relax in her fresh, white linen. She just hoped Andres wouldn't barge in and discover her not working.

She yawned and stretched her hands before removing her clothes and slipping into her cosy bed. She inhaled the fresh scent and immediately relaxed.

Mrs Whittle had changed the bed as per her monthly schedule and glared at her with disapproval. Melissa doubted that Andres had shared the details of their arrangement with Mrs Whittle, whereas her disapproval would probably be justified.

Even through the fresh linen, she could still smell Hugo's scent in the air, which played with her mind. She felt hot and feverish between the covers and inhaled Hugo's scent on top of her lungs. Her hand searched its way over her body and pinched her nipple just as Hugo had done some weeks ago. Her other hand found its way toward her legs, and she gasped out loud when she felt the moisture between her legs.

"Oh my God!

She made rhythmic movements with her hand and bit her lip as another orgasm approached fast, and as the climax washed over her, she felt embarrassed with Hugo's name on her lips.

She quickly jumped out of bed and opened the window to allow the air to filter into the room.

I must be out of my mind.

Luckily, Andres hadn't barged into the room, Melissa thought and eyed at the door whilst dressing up again.

Suddenly, the thought of Andres made Melissa realise that he had been less demanding for days and often let Melissa sleep all night without troubling her. Melissa frowned and left the room to look for him. Although Andres made her life nearly impossible, she did worry as he was still in his recovery period.

As she entered the living room, she found Andres snoring on the sofa with a half-empty bottle of Jack Daniels in front of him. Melissa lifted the glass from his hand and covered his lap with a grey blanket from one of the armchairs. She reclined in the chair farthest from the sofa and stared outside.

Despite only being 5 pm, darkness had fallen outside, and the wind forced the trees to smack against the windows.

Perfect weather for bad decisions, Melissa thought as she impulsively poured herself a glass of whiskey.

She took a short sip and shivered when the strong liquid burned her throat and stomach, but after a few moments, its warmth relaxed her, and she allowed her mind to drift away.

She remembered an event years ago when she had only been sixteen-years-old.

She was sitting in the local library when the heavy double doors burst open, making way for a tall figure followed by sarcastic mocking.

"Stupid four eyes! Shouldn't you go back to your country or learn to speak English properly?"

Melissa heard the loud laughter and glanced outside to see a group of boys mocking Hugo with Andres as their ringleader. "I still can't believe we are twins or even share a mother!"

Andres' hurtful words must have stung, Melissa thought and turned to look at Hugo. She gave him a shy smile, but he quickly pulled his face away and made his way between the bookshelves so Melissa couldn't see him.

Andres wasn't completely wrong; the brothers were nothing alike. While Andres was a bulky, captain of the cricket team, Hugo hid behind his thick glasses and simple polo shirt, spending most of his time with his mother at the Ferrero estate. That's why the heavy Hispanic accent had stuck with him, not with Andres, Melissa had thought.

She continued her book and experienced the feeling of being watched, so she lifted her gaze to find Hugo staring at her from between the bookshelves. When she raised her eyebrows at him, he didn't pull his gaze away. Instead, he looked right into her eyes, but Melissa couldn't read them. Just as quickly, the moment had been gone, and he had marched away from the library, slamming the doors after him, making everyone else jump.

Soon after the incident, Melissa left for university and never saw him until now, nearly ten years later.

"What are you doing here?" Mrs Whittle questioned, disrupting Melissa's memory.

Without looking at her, Melissa finished her drink and stood from the armchair. "Good evening to you too, Mrs Whittle, I was just warming up in front of the fire, that's all."

Mrs Whittle tilted the bottle on the table and shot Melissa a disapproving glance. "I take it it's you who keeps him drinking?"

Melissa scoffed at the accusation. "No, Mrs Whittle, he got into this state on his own. I found him like this and just removed the glass from his hand so he wouldn't spill the whiskey on the sofa."

Melissa didn't know why she still felt obliged to explain herself to Mrs Whittle as she had clearly decided a long time ago that Melissa was the source of all evil in Andres's life, even though she had been completely clueless about the accident until she had attended Patrick's funeral, which felt like ages ago.

Mrs Whittle nodded and dug her chubby arms under Andres' armpits.

"We need to escort him upstairs and help him to bed," Mrs Whittle said.

Melissa hurried over to Andres and Mrs Whittle, and together, they lifted his unconscious body into his wheelchair.

It must be so hard for him, Melissa thought, and she caressed his cheek.

As he slept, Andres looked so much like Hugo, and Melissa questioned whether she would be able to tell the difference between the two of them.

Melissa and Mrs Whittle stood in the lift with Andres and wheeled him to his bedroom. Mrs Whittle hustled around him like a mother, making sure he had a glass of water and a couple of aspirins next to him in case he woke up in the night. Melissa removed his jumper and slipped his pyjama top over him.

"I don't think he will last long like this," Mrs Whittle confessed once they had finished.

"Why do you say that?" Melissa asked, surprised.

Mrs Whittle stared at Andres and sniffled. "Because he is not eating or exercising his body. He is only drinking heavy spirits and staying inside the house. This kind of life would bring anyone to their knees – wheelchair or not."

Melissa looked at Andres with new eyes. "Now that you mention it, he hasn't called for me for a while now."

Mrs Whittle nodded. "He has spent most evenings in his office drinking. I've taken him upstairs and put him to sleep every night."

"I'm sorry you have gone through all that trouble alone. You should have let me know and I would have helped you."

Mrs Whittle gave Melissa a sharp look. "Well, Mrs Ferrero seems to be more interested in her secret visitor rather than *her husband*."

Unintentionally, Melissa blushed and stared at her feet. "It's a private matter that involves Andres as well, so I'm only complying with his wishes."

Mrs Whittle huffed and opened her mouth to object, but Andres erupted into a loud coughing fit that sounded like he had heavy mucus in his throat.

"That can't be good," Melissa said, looking for an answer in the housekeeper's eyes.

Mrs Whittle shook her head, unsurprised. "He has been like this for days. I've dressed him in flannel instead of silk so he is not too cold, but I'm afraid his current lifestyle is not helping at all."

Melissa nodded as Mrs Whittle motioned for them to leave the room and let him rest. She quickly wished her husband goodnight and returned to her own room.

At this point, the heavy drink had made her joints relax and her mind drowsy. She yawned loudly and changed into silk pyjamas.

The temperature had dropped over the last few nights and Melissa shivered. For a second, she played with the idea of entering Andres' room to steal one of his flannel pyjamas when she noticed a flash on her phone.

She checked the screen and discovered ten messages and several missed calls from an unknown number.

Lizzy, it's a shame that you think closing your laptop is going to prevent me from speaking to you. All I want to know is, how are you? Let me know, Hugo

The next message had arrived twenty minutes after the first one, and Hugo had sent the rest in three-minute intervals.

Melissa, I've now asked three times NICELY, but you've ignored me on purpose. Can you please get back to me? Hugo

Melissa, this is ridiculous, all I want is to be nice to you. Please just send me a short message to let me know that you are ok. Hugo

Then the messages took a different tone.

Melissa, you get back to me right now or I'll come over tonight. Hugo

Ok, your attitude has left me with no choice. See you soon! Hugo

I'm on my way. Hugo

When she read the last message, someone knocked on the front door downstairs. Melissa hurled her morning gown over her shoulders and ran to her bedroom door, just in time to hear his footsteps on the staircase.

"Melissa, let me in, now!" Hugo demanded, slamming his fist on her locked door.

Melissa cleared her throat and exhaled. "Hugo, go away. I'm not decent and I want to go to sleep."

"I've seen you indecent before!" Hugo said. "I order you to open this door, now!"

Melissa ignored Hugo's pleas and stayed silent.

The door was made of old wood and wouldn't break no matter how much Hugo hit it with his fists and feet, Melissa knew it and exhaled, knowing that she would be safe from his torment, *for now*.

"*Lizzy*, please open the door for me. I just want to *see you*," Hugo begged. "I just want to make sure you're ok, without any problems. I swear."

Melissa rolled her eyes and said, "I'm perfectly fine, Hugo, now please leave. I want to go to sleep!"

"Then let me *see you*. That's all I'm asking," Hugo pleaded, and he reduced his voice to a whisper. "Are you wearing the pyjamas I saw in your closet the other night?"

Melissa glanced at her closet and noticed her nightwear through the crack in the door. She gasped with embarrassment and blushed from the idea of Hugo rummaging through her things.

"That's not your business!" Melissa hissed. "Please leave before you wake up the whole house!"

As Melissa finished her sentence, she heard Mrs Whittle summoning the security guard and the area outside her door fell silent. She pressed her ear to the door to listen for any more voices or movement when Hugo appeared from the doorway that connected to Andres' room.

Melissa flinched at the sight of him.

"Are you crazy? When someone doesn't open the door for you, it means they don't want to see you!" Melissa hissed, trying to keep her voice down and not wake up Andres.

No matter how much he had demanded her to sleep with his brother, the scene he would witness now would no doubt give him the impression of a lover's spat, which couldn't be further from the truth.

Hugo looked bewildered. Melissa tried to avoid his gaze, but she couldn't help but admire his messy hair and chiselled jaw. Her eyes cast down to his white shirt that revealed the top of his hairy chest and his skinnies that created a noticeable bulge between his legs. The leather jacket finished his bad boy style and Melissa crossed her arms to hide her hardened nipples, but Hugo strode towards her and grabbed her arms.

"When I tell you to jump, you ask how high. I won't take this nonsense behaviour from you, you are my—"

Melissa wrenched her arms free and took a step back.

"That's right, what am I to you? I'm *your brother's wife,* and your presence here is unacceptable," she said and swallowed hard, counting to ten in her mind. "Look, I've already accepted our little arrangement for once a month, but you're damn wrong if you think you can just dash into my bedroom and demand me to play your sick games just because I haven't responded to your messages. I don't care about you, and as soon as I can, I'll be long gone from here. From *you*."

Melissa's outburst made Hugo step back and view her differently for the first time. Something shifted in his eyes as he rubbed his neck and glared at the carpet.

"*Lizzy*, I'm sorry I just…" Hugo said, pausing to find the words. "I just needed to hear *something* from you. I don't think it's too much to ask."

Hugo took a tentative step closer, and Melissa didn't move.

"You're driving me to the edge. This isn't easy for me either and I simply hope that—"

Hugo reached out to touch her when Mrs Whittle and the security guard burst into the room. Mrs Whittle gripped a frying pan in her hand, ready to attack the intruder in her pyjamas.

"Were you going to hit me with that?" Hugo asked, eying the pan in her hand.

Mrs Whittle sighed at the sight of Hugo and lowered the pan. "You two boys are driving me to an early grave, do you hear me!?"

If Melissa hadn't been upset, she would have found the events rather comical, even if Mrs Whittle proceeded to put her down.

"Mr Ferrero, I suggest you leave Mrs Ferrero alone and let her sleep," Mrs Whittle ordered, eying him with disapproval. "I've already called a taxi and booked you a room at the local hotel to ensure you won't drive your motorcycle back in the state you're in."

"State?" Melissa questioned, but she soon understood what the housekeeper meant as she smelled the air around him.

He wreaked of alcohol.

"You drove here drunk? What's wrong with you? Do you have a death wish?" Melissa exclaimed, realising that he must have driven from London even before he had threatened to turn up at the house.

"I told you I would come here if you didn't respond to my texts," Hugo murmured.

The security guard grabbed his shoulder and Hugo unexpectedly let him escort him to the door. He could have easily fought back, and with his build, he would have won, but luckily, he didn't seem to be looking for a fight.

Melissa grinned. "As you can see, I'm just fine, so there was no need to drive here."

Hugo turned back and glared at her with danger in his charcoal eyes.

"Well, I will find out properly in exactly one-hundred-and-forty-four hours," he replied with a sly smile. "Tick tock, my sweet *Lizzy*, *tick tock*."

Melissa's face turned pale as she worked out that one-hundred-and-forty-four hours was just 6 days. Her heart rate quickened, and she broke into a sweat.

"Goodnight, Mrs Ferrero," Mrs Whittle said, and she closed the door that connected to Andres' room.

Melissa didn't feel drowsy anymore. On the contrary, she felt awake more than ever, so she braved a cold shower and eventually drifted into a restless sleep.

15 CHAPTER

Hugo woke up with a splitting headache.

He parted his eyes and glanced around the room only to discover that it was a far cry from his comfortable bedroom at home.

"Crap," he muttered as he recalled the last night's events.

Double crap.

The last night hadn't gone exactly to plan.

It all started with an innocent email correspondence at the office as he had seen Melissa's green status on outlook when Gloria had copied him into one of the many emails she had sent to Melissa. He hadn't been able to resist and reach out to her, but her lack of response had triggered something dark in him. Contrary to his normal behaviour, he had opened a bottle of Jack Daniels and sat down to wait for Melissa to respond. The minutes had turned to hours and Melissa's status had finally turned yellow, indicating that she was not at her desk anymore. It had made Hugo furious.

He had quickly checked the distance to her house, and without further thought, jumped on his motorcycle and rode to her house as quickly as possible. He hadn't expected to find her so defensive or wake up Mrs Whittle with their lover's spat. His only purpose had been to see her and make sure she was ok, and when he had seen her, Hugo had had no problem letting the security escort him out of the house.

He was lucky to have ridden his bike drunk without getting caught. He was a skilful driver and didn't doubt his ability to manage the vehicle after a couple of drinks, but this time, he had definitely crossed the line.

He cursed Melissa and her influence on him once more and got out of bed. He marched to the shower and let the ice-cold water whip his body. He didn't have spare clothing, so he pulled his old gear on and walked out of the hotel.

"Mr Ferrero?"

"Yes?"

"Your taxi is ready for you, Sir."

Hugo watched as the man opened the car door for him and jumped inside.

"Mrs Whittle sent you, I assume?"

"Yes, Sir. I have been waiting outside of the hotel since the morning for you to wake up."

"Good old Mrs Whittle, she doesn't leave anything to chance, does she?" Hugo grinned.

The driver checked his reflection in the front mirror and smiled. "No, Sir."

Hugo leaned back on his seat and silence fell in the car. His phone flashed and he could see the office number calling.

Gloria, he thought and hit the response button. "Yeah?"
"What the hell happened to you yesterday, Hugo Ferrero?! The receptionist tells me you left drunk riding your bike, this better be a poor joke."

Hugo grinned. "I'm afraid not, love. I'm in Canford Cliffs."

A long pause fell on the phone.

"What happened?"

"Nothing, I just went to the mansion to check up on…" He

paused. "…My brother."

"Liar."

"Guilty as charged." Hugo smiled.

"Look, Hugo, I may never understand your obsession with your brother's wife, but you need to fix it quickly. It's Wednesday morning and you're not in the office. There are a lot of people counting on you, and at the moment, you're not giving me your best."

"I know, love."

"Then stop disappointing me, Hugo."

They ended the conversation as he arrived at the main gate of Ferrero Mansion. The driver rang the intercom and the old rusty gate slowly opened, letting them inside.

Hugo jumped out and handed some cash to the driver. "No, Sir, I have been paid for all day as the requester didn't know what time you would be waking up."

Looks like Mrs Whittle doesn't know me that well, after all, he thought and pushed the cash back into his pocket.

"Why don't you spend it with your family, mate? I'm good."

"Are you sure, Sir?"

"Positive."

"Thank you so much, Sir. I don't know what to say."

Hugo smiled. "There is no need to say anything, just enjoy the day."

The driver broke into a wide smile. "I will do, Sir. Have a good day!"

"Yeah, same to you, mate."

Hugo glared at the main entrance and played with the idea of knocking on the door and joining Melissa and his brother for breakfast, but he was afraid that he wouldn't be able to control himself and say something to either of them.

To hell with them both.

Hugo made his way to the back of the mansion where he had left his motorcycle. The bike and helmet were exactly where he had left them the night before. He cleared his hair from his forehead when he noticed a pair of blue eyes staring at him from the window.

Melissa.

She was still in her nightgown with messy hair as if she had been wallowing in bed. He raised his hand to greet her, but she quickly hid behind the curtains. Hugo lowered his hand and waited for a minute to see another glimpse of her, but the window remained empty.

His mind darkened as he felt the familiar feverish longing for her petite frame next to his.

How well they fit together, he thought and felt the front of his skinnies tighten again.

Very soon.

He closed his leather jacket, placed the helmet on his head and hopped onto his motorcycle. His muscular arms bulged as he started the engine and drove away from the main gate.

***

Melissa remained in the corner of her room to ensure that Hugo couldn't see her from his side mirrors. He looked dangerous and sinfully sexy, his hair hiding his left eye and his chin covered with a black 5-o'clock shadow.

Primitive and wild, Melissa thought as an unnoticeable gasp escaped from her lips.

Without any intention, she couldn't *wait* for the next days to pass.

16 CHAPTER

The days flew by quicker than Melissa had hoped, and on the night she had been dreading, she heard a weak knock on her bedroom door. Surprised, she walked to her door and raised an eyebrow when Andres wheeled inside.

"Looks like people do learn. Thanks for knocking on the door instead of barging in."

"If your jokes are of the same quality as this, I'm not surprised that my brother doesn't find you interesting at all," Andres responded and stopped in front of her.

He had changed into his formal dinner attire and combed his black hair back from his face. His chin glowed after a fresh shave, but his eyes remained tired and heavy with dark circles dropping underneath.

Melissa sighed and left the door open. "Is there something I can do for you, Andres?"

"I expect to see you in the main dining room at seven o'clock sharp, don't be late."

Melissa's face fell. "But that's in less than twenty minutes! I won't have time to shower, let alone reapply my make-up."

Andres tilted his head. "Oh, that's just too bad. You'll just have to impress my brother with whatever you're wearing now, but don't worry, I can guarantee that whatever you wear won't make a difference compared to his gorgeous girlfriend."

Melissa let out a frustrated cry. "But we never eat that early, why would you change the time like this without letting me know?"

"Well, today we do, and the longer you stand here arguing with me, the less time you have to prepare," he said and turned to leave the room.

Melissa closed the door quickly and hurried to the shower. She wouldn't have time for make-up.

Melissa arrived in the dining room a couple of minutes late to find Hugo and Andres waiting for her. Hugo stood up as she entered the room and nodded for her to sit down. The polite gesture made her blush, and she glared down at the tapered trousers she had paired with a cashmere cardigan and comfortable slip-ons. She hadn't had the time for make-up and had only briefly brushed her hair.

She sat down, and to her surprise, Andres made no remarks about her outfit. Instead, he gestured for the waitress to start serving the meal.

During dinner, Melissa shot several concerned glances his way, watching him playing with his food, glugging several glasses of whiskey and smoking a cigar, which only made his cough worse. Melissa could hear the mucus accumulating in his airways.

"Melissa, Andres, is there something you want to tell me?" he questioned, crossing his arms with frustration.

Andres' drowsiness made him lower his head on the table and Hugo turned his questioning gaze to Melissa.

"Well, now that you mention it, I'm slightly worried about Andres. He seems more off than usual," Melissa explained. "Less sulky and mean."

At first, Melissa thought she had detected a hint of jealousy in

Hugo's face, but his features softened, and he sighed with sarcastic relief.

"Well, it's nice to see that you two are finally connecting. My part will soon be made redundant, and I'll be able to return to my Gloria. It has been a hell trying to comply with my brother's wishes and keep up the two relationships."

Encouraged by the wine, Melissa raised her eyebrows.

"I didn't know we even had a relationship. I thought we were just…" Melissa motioned her hand in the air as if to think of an appropriate word, when she snapped her fingers and said, "Fucking."

For the first time, Hugo smirked and shifted in his seat, completely caught off guard.

One for me, she thought.

Hugo's stare intensified and he leaned closer to her over the table. "If you like dirty talk, all you'd have to do is ask."

Melissa gasped and a passionate tension built between them. Her worry for Andres disappeared and her mind drifted to something much darker. She held Hugo's gaze until Mrs Whittle entered the dining room to escort Andres back to his bedroom. He waved his hands in protest and Hugo jumped up to assist her.

"I'll carry him," Hugo said as he was clearly unable to hold himself on his chair.

Melissa watched him carry Andres out of the room and sighed when they were out of sight. Andres hadn't hired extra staff for the night, so she gathered up the dishes. After loading everything into the dishwasher, Mrs Whittle popped her head around the kitchen door.

"Mrs Ferrero, you shouldn't bother yourself with the housework. That's my job unless you're unhappy with the way I do it."

Melissa smiled. "I know, Mrs Whittle, and I truly appreciate all the work you do around the house, but Andres has required more of your attention than usual, so I thought I'd express my gratitude by helping out a little bit."

Out of nowhere, Mrs Whittle's eyes filled with tears. "Thank you, dear, it has been a rather challenging month and I'm getting increasingly worried about Andres – Mr Ferrero, I mean. His behaviour has been less intense lately."

Melissa nodded and a comfortable silence fell between them for the first time since they had met. Despite Mrs Whittle's initial hostility towards her, Melissa didn't take joy in seeing her upset. She placed her hand on Mrs Whittle's shoulder and gave her a reassuring smile.

"I'm going to turn in for the night if you don't mind. Thank you once again for your support," Mrs Whittle said, and she disappeared from the room.

Melissa made herself a green tea and waited for it to cool down in the kitchen.

If Hugo remained in the house, he would have to wait. But surely Hugo would have had better things to do with Gloria being back from her travels, so Melissa doubted that he had stayed just for her.

Half an hour later, Melissa washed up the cup in the sink and left it to air dry on the counter. She headed back to her bedroom and flinched at a familiar figure on the bed.

"I thought you would never come up!" Hugo said in a low voice.

Melissa eyed his open shirt and raised her brow at his exposed chest.

"What are you doing here?" Melissa asked, biting her lip and scanning the room for a quick escape route.

Hugo moved onto her bed and leaned on his arm. "I've been waiting for you. It's that time of the month again."

Hugo cast an eye over Melissa's body and an irresistible sensation pulsed between her legs. Her nipples hardened underneath her lacy bra, and she covered her chest with her arms.

Hugo laughed. "It looks like you missed me at least a little bit."

"Don't flatter yourself, it's cold in here," Melissa replied.

Hugo jumped up from the bed and strode over to Melissa. "Well, let me be the judge of that."

Hugo lowered his lips to touch hers, but Melissa turned her head away.

"I don't think Andres would want this anymore. Maybe we should wait until he can clearly express his mind," Melissa suggested, stepping back against the wall.

Hugo's excitement vanished and his eyes flared with fury. "My brother has clearly stated what he wants, so I'm complying with his wishes. Come here, now."

Melissa stayed still, but Hugo bridged the gap between them in two steps and trapped her against the wall. He gripped her waist and thrust himself against her. Melissa felt the swollen bulge between his legs but resisted the urge to jerk her hips back at him.

"Don't play games with me, *Lizzy*, there's no need," Hugo murmured as he nibbled on the side of her neck, leaving a red mark. "It tears me apart having to hold back from stripping you every time I see you. I just want to worship your body like no one else ever has before."

Hugo groaned into her ear and Melissa's knees weakened beneath her. "For the past few weeks, I haven't been able to stop thinking about you and the sweet scent of your pussy when I swirled my tongue inside it. You have made me a savage."

His raw, yet emotional confession forced an excitable smile onto Melissa's face, and she let her body take over. She pulled him into a tight embrace, and he slid his hands over her buttocks. Hugo lifted her against the wall and swirled his tongue inside Melissa's mouth. Melissa gasped with excitement, but Mrs Whittle destroyed their heated moment with her screams.

"Someone please help, he is going to choke!"

Hugo peeled away from Melissa with such speed that she had a hard time catching her breath. The pair sped into Andres' room and gathered around his bed, but there was nothing any of them could do.

Mrs Whittle wailed against Hugo's open chest, and everyone glared at Andres' unconscious body. His eyes were empty, and his breathing had stopped.

He was gone.

17 CHAPTER

Melissa stood paralysed when the paramedics inspected Andres's body. They arrived within ten minutes even though Hugo had told them there was no hurry anymore.

"When did you find him like this?"

"Literally fifteen minutes ago," Hugo responded, trying to keep his voice from breaking.

"And were you the first to find him?"

Hugo shook his head and pointed at Mrs Whittle who sat on the armchair in the corner, staring in front of her. She hadn't spoken since she had called Melissa and Hugo to the room.

The paramedic approached her and knelt in front of her. "Madam, did you find Mr Ferrero unconscious or was he still conscious when you arrived?"

Mrs Whittle didn't react, and Melissa's heart squeezed. She approached her, but Hugo motioned Melissa to sit down and walked over to the old housekeeper, embracing her into his arms. He whispered something into her ear and gently caressed her grey hair. The housekeeper sobbed and blew her nose on an old-fashioned handkerchief before speaking to the paramedics.

Melissa watched them silently and part of her envied the way Hugo comforted Mrs Whittle. She hugged herself and shivered. She didn't remember the last time she had felt so alone.

"Are you Mrs Ferrero?"

Melissa blinked. "Pardon?"

The paramedic gently shook her shoulder. "Madam, can you confirm if you are Mrs Ferrero?"

Melissa nodded. "Yes, yes I am."

"I will need to see some form of ID, and we will also need to know what you would like us to do with your husband's body. If you have his medical record number and instructions in the case of death, that would be helpful too."

"Here is her ID, and I will email our family doctor to let him know," Hugo said, handing Melissa's driving license to the paramedic. "He can pass on all the information you need."

Melissa glanced over to Mrs Whittle who continued to speak to the other paramedic. Melissa had no idea how Hugo had had time to hear their conversation and pick up her handbag, but secretly, she was happy for him to take control of the situation.

"Thank you, that's all I need, Sir," the paramedic said and handed her driving license back to Hugo. "Again, I'm so sorry for your loss."

"Thank you," Hugo responded, and slipped Melissa's driving license back into her handbag.

. Melissa tried to take the handbag from Hugo, but he shot a sharp look at her, so Melissa gave up. She was not in the right frame of mind to argue with him.

"Since we do not suspect a crime here, we will not be taking Mr Ferrero with us, so your next step is to call the funeral services or your insurance to deal with his body."

"Already done. We are waiting for them to arrive at any minute," Hugo said, and Melissa wondered again how Hugo was able to remain efficient in such a situation.

The paramedics left and silence fell …until someone else knocked on the door.

"I'll get it!" Melissa yelled and hurried downstairs.

She couldn't stay in Andres's room for a minute longer.

Two men and a priest arrived. Melissa showed them upstairs and they greeted Hugo.

After a short chat, the two men proceeded to lift Andres's body to the metallic bar where a black bag was laid open.

The closing of the heavy zip sounded final.

"Melissa, can you please take Mrs Whittle downstairs and help her to prepare some chamomile tea for all of us? I'll escort the team outside," Hugo said.

Melissa blinked as if Hugo had spoken a foreign language.

"We will do, Mr Ferrero. Thank you for dealing with this," Mrs Whittle said and grabbed Melissa's arm.

Melissa glanced at the black bag once more and followed Mrs Whittle downstairs.

That was the last night she saw her husband.

After the funeral services left with Andres's body, Melissa finally broke into tears. She collapsed onto the sofa in the living room and buried her face into her palms, letting her sobs shake her body.

Melissa tried to sip her chamomile tea, but all she could taste were her salty tears. Part of her felt bad for not crying sooner, but it had been difficult when all the arrangements and Mrs Whittle's distress had taken such a priority, and she appreciated how tough it must be to lose someone you've looked after for years.

On some level, Melissa should have been pleased that Andres had died. His death had freed her, but the image of his empty body made the tears swamp her face, and the guilt from how she had wrapped her legs around Hugo's waist just seconds before Andres had passed made her feel sick.

"You shouldn't be here alone."

Melissa turned her head to see Hugo enter the living room.

His eyes were puffy from crying and a hint of whiskey surrounded him. Hugo sat in the armchair next to her and Melissa glanced at his profile. There was nothing left of the man she had seen in her room just minutes before they had stormed into Andres's room. All evidence of their passionate encounter had been wiped away.

He continued to stare forward with empty eyes, making him appear more powerful than ever before. Hugo's silence sent chills through Melissa's body, and she jumped a little when he faced her.

"You should go and pack, we are leaving."

Seconds passed before Melissa registered what he had said.

"What?" she cried.

Hugo's jaw tensed. "Pack your things, we are leaving."

"I heard you the first time, but where are we going?"

"London. The doctors want to carry out an autopsy on Andres' body to determine the cause of his death," Hugo replied.

"Do they have reason to doubt a natural death?" Melissa asked, surprised.

Hugo's nostrils flared and his eyes burned with rage. "Well, let's just say you're lucky to have me as your alibi for at least half an hour before his death."

Melissa knitted her eyebrows and gaped. "You've got to be joking! I wouldn't hurt a fly!"

She stood from her seat and glowered at Hugo.

"Sit down, I haven't finished yet," Hugo demanded, ignoring her outburst.

Melissa scoffed. "You are wrong if you think I'm going to sit here and listen to your accusations! You were there with me the whole time, and I find it hurtful that you even *think* I have anything to do with your brother's death. On the contrary, I told you that he had seemed strange for the past few weeks."

Melissa turned to walk away, but Hugo leapt from the chair and grabbed her wrist.

"I told you to sit down, I haven't finished yet and it's important that you listen to me."

"Spit it out then," Melissa hissed, crossing her arms.

Hugo cleared his throat. "As I said, pack your things because we are going back to London. They are moving Andres' body tonight to St. Thomas Hospital. The autopsy is meant to take place in two days, so the report will be released within a week. Before it happens, you will stay with me in my London house so I can keep my eye on you."

Melissa opened her mouth to protest but thought better of it. The idea of staying alone at the mansion didn't feel right to her, and if she stayed at her father's house, the nosy locals would never leave her alone. She didn't have a flat in London anymore as she had given it away when she had got married, but she would figure it out.

"Give me twenty minutes and meet me downstairs," she said and headed to her room.

In less than fifteen minutes, Melissa had packed her two suitcases. She had first arrived at the mansion with very little, and she didn't plan to take anything Andres had bought for her either, but when she glanced at her open closet, she spotted the expensive lingerie. She ambled over to close the door, but she took a moment to let the delicate fabric caress her skin for the last time.

"Take them all."

Melissa jumped and whipped around. Hugo stood in the doorway and watched her every move.

She blushed. "I don't think there is any use for these anymore."

Hugo shook his head. "On the contrary, I'm sure there is plenty of use for such beautiful clothing. Take everything from your closet."

"No, I couldn't, it's too much, I wouldn't dare."

Hugo huffed and charged toward her. "Why do I always have to fight to get anything through to you?" He slammed the closet door fully open and ripped the clothes off their hangers. "These were bought for you; anything less would be an insult to the next woman wearing them!"

For a second, Melissa pictured Gloria wearing the delicate garments and a range of feelings surged through her, jealousy being the main one.

"Ok, I'll take them," she agreed, placing them into her suitcase. Who knew, maybe she could find a use for them now she had been freed.

"Got everything?" Hugo asked.

Melissa nodded and Hugo lifted both suitcases from the bed as if they weighed nothing. She followed him out of the room and closed the door behind them without looking back.

The two of them headed for the entrance hall when something suddenly occurred to Melissa as she tried to ignore Hugo's masculine scent.

"What about Mrs Whittle?" she asked.

"I've sent her to her male companion's place downtown," Hugo explained. "She will be fine."

Melissa raised her eyebrows. "A male companion?"

The corner of Hugo's mouth twitched into a smile. "You think you were the only one with something going on?"

Melissa blushed and giggled. "No, I just never thought she would be in any relationship as she is quite…"

Melissa searched for the right word, but Hugo beat her to it.

"Demanding?" he offered.

Melissa smiled, relieved. "Yes."

Hugo shrugged and motioned for Melissa to step outside. She waited as Hugo locked the front door and nodded towards the black Mercedes.

"I'm not sure you're in the right mindset to drive today," Melissa said, but Hugo continued to load the suitcases into the boot and prompted her to get inside the car.

"Nah, driving helps me to relax. Don't worry, I'm a safe driver."

Melissa hesitated, but after a moment, she nodded and got into the passenger side.

Hugo pulled away from the main gate and Melissa exhaled as she finally left her horrifying marriage behind.

***

Melissa opened her droopy eyes as Hugo lifted her from the car seat, and she snuggled into his warm body all the way to the freshly made bed in the apartment. Hugo's scent made her skin tingle and the hairs on her arms raised. Without thinking, Melissa planted soft kisses along Hugo's neck, and he moaned with pleasure until their lips finally met once again. Hugo's muscles tensed as he groaned into their passionate kiss, and he grabbed her bum to pull her closer.

Melissa tugged on his white shirt and Hugo understood the gesture. He unbuttoned the front with speed and Melissa explored his sun-kissed chest with her lips, trailing towards his stomach.

"Melissa, if you're not serious, please stop," Hugo groaned and grabbed Melissa's face. "Please tell me to stop and I'll stop. We are not in the right mind for this now."

Melissa's mouth quivered into a mischievous smile, and she whispered, "Please don't stop, let me love you if only this one time."

Hugo returned her smile and removed his trousers. Melissa dropped her cardigan to the floor and slipped off her trousers and lace panties, exposing her bare skin. Hugo inhaled at the sight of Melissa's body and pulled her back onto the bed. He plunged between her legs and let himself own her like no one else ever had.

18 CHAPTER

As the morning sun glistened through the window, Melissa's stomach growled with hunger. She glared underneath the duvet and eyed Hugo's naked body, intertwined with hers. Melissa tried to wriggle herself free without waking him up, but the man behind her had the instinct of an animal.

"Go back to sleep," Hugo murmured without opening his eyes.

Melissa smiled at Hugo's hoarse morning voice and noticed her clothes in a disorganized heap on the floor. She sighed with relief and hurried to the en-suite. She admired the expensive soaps dotted around the bathroom and hopped into the glass shower to wash off the fatigue in her joints.

As she shampooed her hair and enjoyed the heat of the water, Melissa's chest tightened with guilt. Despite losing Andres less than twelve hours ago, *she* had lured Hugo into sleeping with her, but she blushed as she recalled screaming his name as they climaxed together. Melissa had been loud, and in the heat of the moment, Hugo had placed his mouth on top of hers, inhaling her screams before she had fallen asleep in his arms.

As Melissa smirked at the memory, a breeze of cold air entered the bathroom.

The shower door slid open, and Hugo stepped inside, fully naked.

"Excuse me, have we met?" Melissa teased, staring at Hugo's aroused package.

Hugo continued to wash and snigger at Melissa. "I'm not sure, you tell me, or maybe I was just dreaming last night."

Melissa blushed. "Oh, that must be it then. I was *sleeping*."

Hugo rolled his eyes and grabbed the shower head from above them. He playfully pointed the water at Melissa's face, and she covered her face with her palms.

Hugo's mouth quivered into a mischievous smile, and he stepped forward. He reconnected the shower head and grabbed Melissa's waist.

"It's too late to be shy, *Lizzy*. We have seen each other in all possible ways," Hugo said, ogling her body.

"That's not the point, cut it out and stop looking at me like that," Melissa exclaimed, trying to cover her private areas.

Hugo pushed Melissa against the wet wall and thrust his throbbing manhood against her body.

"Or what?" he challenged.

Melissa inhaled as his body rubbed against her hypersensitive skin. "Just stop! We are not in the right mind for this now!"

Hugo guffawed. "I think that's my line from last night, why don't you invent your own, *amor mio*."

Melissa furrowed her brow. "What does that mean?"

"Why don't you look in the Spanish dictionary? I'm sure I have one here next to *Kamasutra*."

Melissa's cheeks reddened and she ducked under Hugo's arm. This type of intimate talk was new to her, and she didn't know how Hugo expected her to react.

"I need to go," Melissa murmured.

She opened the glass door and covered her hot body with the fluffy white towel on the rail. Hugo watched her disappear back into the bedroom, and Melissa changed into a casual outfit from one of her suitcases.

While Hugo finished up in the bathroom, Melissa decided to explore the rest of the house.

She ambled through the main corridor and noticed that the house had three bedrooms, a dining room, a living room, and an open-plan kitchen. The living room had a massive set of windows that looked out onto the River Thames.

Melissa eyed the framed photographs that adorned the walls and smiled at Hugo with her mother in different countries. None of the photos included Andres or their father, which made a lot of sense to Melissa.

"Did you find anything to eat yet?" Hugo asked from behind her.

Melissa jumped and turned around.

"No, I haven't looked yet," she said, crossing her arms.

Hugo nodded. "Fair enough, I'll make us a quick breakfast. Then we need to talk."

Melissa followed Hugo through to the kitchen and watched him move effortlessly around the room, bringing all the ingredients together and heating the electric hob. She admired Hugo's broad figure in his black t-shirt and jeans, and an uncontrollable pulsing sensation crept between her legs as she observed his authoritative aura.

Who could say no to him? she wondered.

"I don't know how you like your eggs, but I guessed runny on top," Hugo said as he served a full English breakfast.

Melissa gave a shy smile. "That's actually exactly how I like them."

Hugo beamed and they ate in silence, both in their own thoughts. Melissa eyed Hugo's profile and realised how calm and collected he had been since his brother's death, but the pale skin and dark circles under his eyes reflected his pain. She wanted to reach out and console him, but she didn't want to smother him or remind him of his loss, so she remained in her seat and said nothing.

After breakfast, Hugo served hot drinks and led Melissa to the sofa in the living room, but instead of sitting next to her, he sat on the coffee table in front of her.

"We need to talk," he began, looking into Melissa's eyes.

"I figured as much."

Hugo nodded. "As we know, Andres is dead, but I'm not sure if you were aware of the family arrangements. There is quite an extensive prenuptial agreement that the family lawyers signed long before you two got married, but it protects the family assets to the bone."

Melissa nodded and Hugo continued.

"That means you aren't entitled to any of Andres's fortune whatsoever. You can fight for it, but your chances are slim. Even if you did win the case, it would take years before you saw a dime," Hugo explained, searching Melissa's face. "So, it's unlikely that you'll be able to save your father's home."

Melissa gasped. "How do you know about that?"

Hugo sighed. "He briefly mentioned it to me and then I got confirmation when going through Andres' paperwork. The odd number of monthly transfers caught my eye, so I worked it out."

Melissa's shoulders relaxed. "I'm actually glad you found out as it has been something I wanted to discuss with you, but we never had a perfect time."

She blushed as she realised the reasons *why* they had never had the time to talk. Melissa cleared her throat and Hugo waited for her to resume.

"Anyway, I'm more than happy to leave everything behind and

start working again. The only thing I would like to ask you for is a loan that will settle the debt against my father's house," Melissa said. "Naturally, I would pay it back, but I might need a little bit longer before I'm back on my feet. I could even look for a second job to repay you faster."

"No," Hugo said.

Melissa raised her eyebrows. "What do you mean *no?*"

Hugo's features hardened and he clenched his jaw. "I mean *no*. I'm not going to give you a loan to pay off your father's debt."

Melissa frowned and leaned forward. "Why not? Don't you trust me enough to pay you back? We can sign official loan papers if that puts your mind at ease?"

Hugo shook his head. "I'm not interested in loaning you money, and it has nothing to do with you paying me back or not. There is simply no benefit for me in the arrangements. No gain at all."

Melissa covered her mouth with dread and swallowed hard. "What should I do then?"

Melissa's brain switched into fifth gear, and she desperately tried to think of another solution to keep her panic at bay, but she had no possible solutions in her mind. Due to her credit rating, no bank would allow her to take out a personal loan, so Hugo was her only chance.

"*What* do I do?" Melissa pressed in a firm tone.

"We could continue Andres's arrangement," Hugo suggested.

Melissa jerked her head up. "Excuse me?"

"You heard me," he said, his gaze intensifying. "Obviously, there would be a slight change to our previous arrangement. I would expect you to live here with me and be available at *any time*, not just once a month. And I would expect this arrangement to produce a child."

Melissa shook her head. "No, this is insane! We don't know each other! Hell, we don't even *like* each other. I was your brother's wife!"

"All the more reason as no one would ever question anything - you are already Mrs Ferrero."

"You are insane! How can you expect me to bring a child into this twisted circumstance? No, I won't do it, you can't make me!"

Melissa stood up and wiped her sweaty hands onto her leggings.

Hugo tensed his jaw. "You didn't seem to have any problem not using protection last night."

Melissa's skin turned pale. "You can't be sure that last night got me pregnant. Many women take months to conceive."

Hugo leaned back and relaxed his body. "Fine with me, but your father's house will go on sale tonight."

Melissa scowled. "Why are you doing this to me? Aren't there enough women out there who will bend over when you ask them to? Why do you have to bully me into submission?"

Hugo got to his feet and circled the table between them. He crouched before her and gently grabbed her wrist.

"Because there is something in you, Melissa, that I need more than air to breathe," Hugo whispered, leaning forward to kiss her. "Think about it. If you think Andres was bad, trust me when I say that you don't want to make an enemy of me."

Hugo's words sent an ominous shiver down Melissa's spine, and he held Melissa's stare before he stood and left her in the living room.

She buried her face into her palms and allowed fresh tears to flood her face.

Her sacrifice for her father's sake had been short-lived, and now, if she accepted Hugo's proposal, she would likely end up in a worse situation than before, and she didn't know if she would survive after Hugo had finished playing with her, but what other choice did she have?

Living with Andres had been the worst few months of her life, but the potential consequences of Hugo's agreement would force them together for the rest of their lives, and knowing Hugo, he would use everything against her in all possible ways, leaving her wrecked and shattered, a ghost of the woman she had once been.

***

After Hugo left the living room, he stormed into his home office door and cursed into the room. He considered taking another cold shower, but he changed his mind after he realised how much he had betrayed his brother. Continuing Andres' arrangement had never occurred to him before, but since his brother's death, Melissa had become a free woman to see, date and live her life beyond the control of the Ferrero family.

Although Hugo often questioned Melissa's morals and found her infuriating, he couldn't imagine life without her. He had been forced to admire her from afar for years, but now he had tasted the forbidden fruit, he just couldn't let her go.

Hugo ignored Melissa's sobs from the living room, but every inch of his body urged him to turn around and console her. He wanted to tell her that everything would be ok and that she was free to go, but he couldn't lose her.

19 CHAPTER

Melissa's sobs slowly died as she pulled herself together.

The freedom she had felt when Andres died shrunk around her as she followed Hugo to his home office. She knocked lightly on the door and waited, but when nobody responded, so she opened the door ajar.

"What do you want, Melissa?"

Melissa pushed the door open and found Hugo sitting in front of his writing desk. The room exuded wealth and power with its Persian carpet and giant furniture.

"I just thought we should continue the conversation if you have time," she said, stepping into the room.

"Have you made a decision yet?"

"No, but…"

"Then there is nothing to discuss."

Melissa ignored Hugo's rejection. "What happens if I say no?"

Hugo leaned back on his chair and watched Melissa. "I would ask you to leave this house immediately. If anything needs agreeing, the communication will take place via our solicitors. You would not hear from or see me ever again."

Melissa gulped. It sounded like all she had ever wanted, but the idea of never seeing Hugo again pained her heart. She dreaded her next question.

"Why won't you ask Gloria to give you a child? Why do you need one from me?"

Hugo's gaze intensified and his jaw line tensed. "My relationship with Gloria is none of your business. I love our relationship just as it is, and I wouldn't change it for anything."

Hearing Hugo defend his relationship with Gloria infuriated Melissa, and she felt a shot of jealousy, which died quickly as she realised that there might be a medical reason behind his request.

"Oh, do you mean Gloria can't have children, is that what this is? Your brother died and now you're looking for a cheap surrogate for her? Well, in that case, I won't even consider your proposal! My children are sacred to me!"

Hugo cursed and strode towards Melissa so quickly that she gasped with fear. He grabbed her waist and pulled her close. "I would never separate a child from her mother, I'm not a monster."

"You could fool me. Your proposal doesn't sound completely sane either."

"And yet, you are considering it, aren't you?" Hugo said, grinning.

Melissa wrenched herself from his embrace. "I'm not! In all seriousness, I'm thinking about how we can keep civilised in a working environment if I say no. Don't forget, I work with Gloria now."

Hugo's expression got serious, and he walked to the window to admire the skyline. "I never mix business and pleasure, Melissa. Any business relationship you have with Gloria remains as it is, I can guarantee you that. Which reminds me, she sends her condolences to you."

Melissa raised her eyebrow. "Oh, I didn't know you had seen her already."

Hugo shook his head. "I spoke to her on the phone last night."

Melissa's mood sank. "Well, I'm glad you have someone to support you too during this difficult time."

Hugo abruptly turned to face Melissa. His jaw tensed and his expression grew cold. "What do you actually need, Melissa?"

Melissa wasn't the type of girl to ask for favours, but this time she didn't have a choice.

"I want you to let me have time to think about your proposal without having to worry about the ongoing repayments of my father's house. You can't expect me to decide right away."

Hugo shook his head. "As I told you, I have no reason to continue the repayments. They will remain on hold until I hear back from you."

"You can't do that; this month is yet to go through!" Melissa cried.

Hugo smiled. "Then that's very unfortunate for you, *my Lizzy*. It looks like you need to make up your mind as soon as possible."

"Look, you are not only asking me to stay with you. You are asking me to give you a child. This is a much bigger commitment than I ever had with your brother."

Hugo's eyes darkened as she strode to Melissa and grabbed her waist. "I don't care what kind of relationship you had with my brother, but I'm sure it was much more than a simple platonic sister-and-brother type of relationship."

If he only knew.

Melissa swallowed the lump in her throat as the familiar masculine scent surrounded her. Now she knew it was pointless to open up to Hugo about her previous relationship with his brother.

"How soon do you need my reply?"

"As soon as possible."

"I'll give you my response in seven days, but before that, can you please make sure the repayment goes through this month? I don't want to beg, but here I'm on my knees in front of you, please have mercy on me, Hugo," Melissa pleaded.

A lonely strand escaped from her messy bun and Hugo brushed it away. The intimacy of the gesture made Melissa's toes curl with pleasure.

"Fine, you have seven days and I'll move the repayment date further, but that's all I can do for you, Melissa. You need to make up your mind as fast as possible for both of our sakes."

Melissa nodded and stepped back from his embrace. "I will give you my reply in seven days. Meanwhile, I noticed you have three bedrooms here, which one do you want me…"

"No."

Melissa paused. "What do you mean?"

"I mean no, you won't move out of my bedroom."

"Hugo, come on. This is hardly an appropriate arrangement so close to your brother's death, besides, you promised me time!"

"Yet, you had no problem hopping in the sack with me last night."

Touché.

His words stung, and Melissa felt worn out. Her defeat must have shown on her face when Hugo suddenly raised her jaw to face him. "You can sleep with me, but I promise I will leave you alone. You don't have to do anything with me unless you want to, of course, are we clear?"

Melissa nodded. "But from now on, we use protection, is that clear?"

The moment the words left her mouth, she could have kicked herself. Hugo's mouth quivered into a mischievous smile. "I thought you wanted me to leave you alone?"

"Of course, I do!"

"Well, make up your mind then!" he said and escorted her out of the room. "As much as this conversation amuses me, I still have work to do."

Melissa left and weighed her options as she opened her laptop and utilised her time by attending to some work matters. The new environment gave her much-needed tranquillity and she lost the track of time… until Hugo knocked on the door with a Chinese take-away. Melissa laughed and closed her laptop.

They ate in the living room and watched old movies, and when it was time to go to bed, they couldn't fight against the attraction that made their bodies melt together and gasp with pleasure. Melissa gave up and let her body join his for the sweet release only he could offer her, leaving her silent whimpers and his loud groans the only witnesses of the night.

20 CHAPTER

"Are you ready to go?" Hugo asked two days later, popping his head into Melissa's room.

Melissa smiled. "Give me five minutes and I'll be ready."

Since Hugo had proposed a new arrangement to Melissa, she had only seen him a couple of times in the corridor and at the dinner table, but as each day passed, he looked more and more like his brother, so much so that Melissa expected him to insult her.

Instead, Hugo had given her until the end of the week to decide her future, and he had honoured his words and not mentioned his proposal once. Still, Melissa had no idea what to decide, but she was running out of time.

Melissa gathered herself and Hugo drove the pair of them to St Thomas Hospital.

"Are you nervous?" Hugo asked as he switched off the engine.

"For what?"

"What the autopsy report might reveal."

Melissa shook her head. "No, I don't have any reason to be."

Hugo glanced at her profile. "Are you nervous about something else then?"

Melissa turned to face him. "Why do you ask?"

"You seem tense."

"Trust me, I'm fine," Melissa said, and after a short pause, she continued. "Well, there is actually something I wanted to mention to you earlier this week."

"What is it?"

"I want to go to my old office and work there for a day."

"No."

"What do you mean no? The autopsy report is released today. I'm at your mercy to pay for my father's house. What more do you need to ensure that I don't run at the first instance?!"

Hugo weighed her words. "Mm, you might be right. It's not the worst option after all. As long as I take you there."

"I didn't expect anything less from you, Sir."

"Stop it or you'll wait in the car."

"Oh, on the contrary, Mr Ferrero. I wouldn't miss this for the world."

Hugo found a parking space and killed the engine. "Off you go then, Mrs Ferrero."

The two of them left the car and headed to the fifth floor to meet Dr Townsend, a family friend and the head of the pathology department.

"Good afternoon, Mr and Mrs Ferrero," Dr Townsend greeted. "Please, take a seat."

Melissa and Hugo sat in the guest chairs in front of Dr Townsend's desk and waited for him to continue. Dr Townsend sighed and glanced between the two of them.

"I appreciate how difficult this must be for you and your wife," he began.

Melissa opened her mouth to clarify that they weren't together, but

Hugo squeezed her hand to keep her quiet. She sank into her seat and Dr Townsend eyed her with suspicion, but Hugo hurried to respond.

"Apologies for my wife, she is a little nervous around this topic."

Hugo squeezed her hand again and Dr Townsend smiled with understanding, oblivious to the deeper meaning behind his grip.

"It's understandable, Mrs Ferrero, but interestingly, a post-mortem examination is one of the most fascinating topics for any pathologist," Dr Townsend replied, and he continued to explain the medical procedure for the autopsy and how they gathered different pieces of evidence for the report.

Melissa listened as much as possible, but she couldn't help but think about how to escape from yet another marital arrangement. She had found it easy to remain indifferent to Andres, even if he had forced her to leave her job and endure multiple daily insults, but it would be completely different with Hugo, especially with children involved. Melissa wouldn't admit it aloud, but she had developed strong feelings for Hugo over time, though, she didn't know if those feelings were enough.

Besides, Gloria continued to lurk behind the scenes like a ghost, completely unaware that they had been sleeping together. Although Melissa had enabled Hugo to cheat on Gloria, she could never imagine sharing him with anyone else, but she struggled with the new agreement idea. How could she agree to continue with Hugo and have a child with him in exchange for money to offset her father's debts? Melissa didn't want to think about it too much, but it sounded too much like prostitution, which made her shiver in her seat.

"*Amor mio*, are you cold?" Hugo asked, wrapping his leather jacket around her shoulders.

Melissa snuggled inside the warm fabric and nodded to thank him.

"Therefore, the sole reason for your brother's death is the chest infection that caused extensive mucus to build up in his lungs."

Hugo gasped and Melissa grabbed his hand to console him.

"Is there anything we could have done?" Hugo questioned, his voice breaking.

Dr Townsend shook his head. "It could have been anything that caused the virus to enter his body: a lack of good nutrition, no exercise, extensive drinking. You name it."

Hugo nodded and rubbed his chin thoughtfully.

"Now, are there any more questions you would like to ask before we continue with the practicalities of moving the body for the funeral?" Dr Townsend asked, closing the paper case in front of him.

"Did he suffer?" Melissa blurted out, causing Hugo to look up at the doctor.

"No, he didn't suffer. The mucus would have built up slowly, so he would have lost consciousness before he died."

As if planned, Melissa and Hugo exhaled with relief at the same time, letting the doctor's reply digest.

After the meeting with Dr Townsend, they left the hospital and headed back to Hugo's car.

"Can you drop me off at my office?" Melissa asked as Hugo turned the key in the ignition.

Hugo nodded and dropped her off at her destination, but before Melissa had the chance to step out of the car, he grabbed her wrist.

"I'll be back in a couple of hours, make sure you are ready by then."

Melissa winced and said, "You know, it wouldn't kill you to be nice to me sometimes."

Hugo let go and Melissa rubbed her skin.

"Go, before I change my mind."

Melissa jumped out of the car and watched him speed away, ignoring the upcoming cars that honked at his reckless driving. She glanced at the darkening sky and entered the office.

***

"Melissa!" Jason chirped as she stepped inside. "Honey, it's so good to see you alive!"

The workplace hadn't changed since Melissa had left over three months ago to marry Andres and work remotely. A few new cubicles had been installed in the open-plan office, but everyone appeared to be just as busy, speaking on the phone and yelling instructions over their cubicle partitions. A couple of her previous colleagues greeted her from their seats, but most others eyed her as if deciding whether she would be a threat to them on the job market.

Melissa chuckled as the familiar energy returned to her body after her three-month hibernation in the mansion.

"I couldn't be happier to be back, Jason! It feels good to see everyone. They seem so busy!"

Jason nodded. "You bet! After we took on Garcia Industries, it has been like this non-stop."

Melissa followed her boss to his office and smiled at a few colleagues along the way.

"I hope there is some work left for me as well, now that I'm back," Melissa joked, but her grin dropped when she noticed her desk next to his in the office.

"Jason, why my things are in here?" she asked, pointing at the bucket of fresh flowers and welcoming card on the desk.

Jason shifted with awkwardness. "*Honey*, I didn't know if you would be coming back, and I needed to make room for the new lads. You had the biggest room in the office, but as it wasn't being used, I had to make the difficult decision and pass it on to other users. I hope you understand."

Jason's decision stung, but Melissa forced a smile. "Not at all, I get it."

Melissa strolled around her boss' office and took a seat at her desk.

"I didn't know I would be placed in the same room as the boss, though. Don't you trust me anymore?" Melissa joked.

Jason stayed silent and pursed his lips with apology.

"I can't believe it, Jason. After getting you the biggest account of your lifetime, you still don't trust me?"

"Well, I didn't know what to think after you started working remotely and then never attending our weekly meetings," Jason admitted, twiddling a pen between his fingers. "But I actually have another reason for moving you into my office."

Melissa raised her eyebrows. "Oh?"

"Well, it's kind of private and non-work related," Jason replied, licking his lips nervously. "I wondered… now that you're newly single and in town again, would you like to see each other officially? I never got the chance to ask you before you married some royalty far away from London."

Melissa widened her eyes and stared at her boss with surprise. She had always admired Jason and had warm feelings toward him, but she had never considered a relationship with him.

"Jason, I can't tell you how flattered I am for your attention, and I'm more than happy to go out with you as a friend, but that's all I have to offer for now," Melissa said.

She beamed with apology in her eyes and touched his snowman tie… he had always had an odd sense of fashion.

"I figured as much," Jason replied, brushing her cheek. "Please let me know if there is anything I can do for you in the meantime."

Melissa gathered her courage and inhaled. *It was now or never.*

"Jason, there might be something I need to ask you," Melissa began, stepping back. "This is embarrassing to even ask, but would you be able to loan me some money to cover some unforeseen debts my father left behind? I know it's very sudden, but I'm planning to work double shifts and get a weekend job to pay it off as soon as possible. We can make the paperwork as tight as you need, I'm open to everything. Sorry to put you on the spot."

After Melissa finished her sentence, a flood of tears surfaced in her eyes and Jason grabbed her in a bear-like hug. "Shh there, *baby girl*, it's ok. Of course, I will loan you money, there is no issue at all."

Melissa lifted her head and stared into his soft eyes. "Really?"

Jason smiled and ruffled her golden locks. "Of course, *silly*. Believe it or not, I don't have many expenses, and my grandmother left me a slice of her heritage when she passed away last year, so trust me, *baby girl,* I'm loaded."

Melissa burst into laughter and wiped the corners of her eyes. "You're impossible, you know that?"

"Who knows, maybe you will be willing to marry me one day," Jason joked, embracing her tighter.

"I'm afraid that will have to wait until *never,*" a hoarse voice snapped from outside the door.

Hugo stepped in. "Oh, did I interrupt a sweet lover's planning? So silly of me, maybe I should come back again once Melissa has paid off the first instalment of her much-needed loan! With open legs as per usual."

Hugo charged toward the pair of them and hurled his hand across Melissa's desk. All of her belongings fell to the floor, including the vase that smashed to pieces.

"I think this desk will do just fine for the first loan instalment, or what you think, Jason, wasn't it?" Hugo sneered.

"How dare you march into my workplace and disrespect me like this!" Melissa barked; her eyes wide with fury.

"Well, I didn't know I had competition, otherwise I would have demanded that you accept my proposal a week ago!"

"I never accepted your terms and conditions anyway," Melissa hissed.

Hugo stepped closer to her and said, "Well, that's something we will learn by end of the month, don't you think?"

Melissa and Hugo glared at each other like bulls ready to charge when Jason's shrill voice filled the air between them.

"Melissa, I thought you said your husband had died?"

Jason pointed at Hugo, but Hugo swung his hand towards him. "Didn't your mother ever tell you that pointing is impolite?"

Melissa rushed between them. "Hugo, stop it right now! Jason, this is my brother-in-law, Hugo, Andres's twin brother."

Hugo nodded. "And we are to be married very soon because she is pregnant."

Jason's eyebrows shot up as he eyed Melissa.

"That's not true at all. Stop it, Hugo, you're embarrassing me!"

"It's irrelevant now because you're never returning to this office again! Pack your things, we are leaving."

Hugo seized her hand, but Melissa yanked herself away from him and stepped back.

"No, I'm not going anywhere! I've just got my job back, so stop telling me what to do!"

Hugo lowered his hand and his gaze intensified. "For the last time, pack your stuff and let's go, *now!*"

"Eh, Hugo, is it?" Jason interrupted with a firm voice. "I'm sure you are used to treating people like this but let me remind you that you're in *my office* now, and here, we treat all staff with respect. If you can't comply with this, I will need to ask you to leave immediately before I call the police. When Melissa is ready to leave, I'm more than happy to take her wherever she wants to go."

Hugo's face turned the colour of blood and he shoved Jason across the desk.

"Jason, no!" Melissa screamed.

She hurried over to him on the floor when two strong arms grabbed her waist.

"Where do you think you're going? I said out!" Hugo roared.

"Let me go! I hate you!" Melissa yelled, struggling to get away.

"This is what you get for playing with fire since you were a teenager!" Hugo hissed as he swung her over his shoulder like a sack of potatoes.

Hugo carried Melissa and her handbag out of the office, and everyone watched the scene from their cubicles, some gaping with shock and others sniggering.

"Let me down now or I swear you will never see me again!" Melissa shouted as they got outside.

Hugo ignored her until he shoved her into the back of his Mercedes. Melissa hurried to the other side to escape, but Hugo had child-proofed both doors.

"Put on your seat belt," Hugo ordered in a calm tone as he started the engine.

He glanced over his shoulder all the way back to his house and walked her inside, keeping his hands around her waist so she couldn't escape. Hugo dragged her into the living room when Melissa pulled away from his reach.

"What do you *want* from me?" she questioned, breaking down into tears.

"What do I *want* from you? I thought I made that clear a week ago."

Melissa shook her head. "No, you gave me an ultimatum, which technically meant that I have no choice but to accept your offer."

Hugo bridged the gap between them, and Melissa inhaled as their bodies touched.

"And you think that slimy chimp is better than me?"

Melissa sniffled and wiped her face. "Well, at least I would be able to maintain my independence with Jason, and I wouldn't have to share him!"

"What do you mean, *share?*" Hugo said, losing sight of the argument.

Melissa huffed and forced back more tears. "Women don't usually like to share their…oh, forget it, it doesn't matter. We are not real anyway, so it would just be best for us to go our separate ways."

"Is that so?" Hugo challenged and planted a soft kiss on her cheek. "Does that feel real enough for you?"

"Hugo, stop it," Melissa said, holding her breath as her body heated with desire.

She lifted her hands onto his shoulders and pulled him in for an embrace.

"Correct me if I'm wrong, but *this* feels *real* to me," Hugo murmured against her lips.

Melissa exhaled deeply and allowed him to kiss her. Hugo's shirt and jeans quickly found their way to the floor… followed by Melissa's blouse.

Hugo grinned and strode towards the bedroom, but in the heat of the moment, Melissa grabbed her shirt and Hugo's car keys from the breakfast bar and legged it from the house.

"Melissa!" Hugo roared as he realised Melissa's plan.

He continued to yell after her, but Melissa slipped into his car and started the engine. The GPS welcomed her as she pressed 'search'. She had no idea where she wanted to go, so she chose the last searched destination.

"Great," she huffed as she saw Gloria's name on the GPS and sped into the night.

21 CHAPTER

"Melissa! What happened to you?" Gloria exclaimed as she opened the front door.

Melissa shivered in her cardigan. "I need to speak to you, it's urgent."

"Sure, come in," Gloria said, her voice still husky from being asleep.

Melissa stepped inside and Gloria led her through the well-lit corridor to the cosy living room. The scent of fresh flowers and different plants filled the room and the large windows looked out onto the River Thames, just like Hugo's flat.

Her occupation makes complete sense now, Melissa thought as she eyed her in the green living room.

Gloria gestured for her to sit down on the white sofa.

"Shall I make you a cup of tea or would you prefer something stronger?" Gloria asked, handing Melissa the fluffy blanket from the sofa.

"Oh, um, a tea's fine, thank you," Melissa replied, snuggling into the blanket.

Gloria nodded and disappeared into the kitchen.

Melissa glanced around the room and noticed the multiple family photographs that adorned the green walls, but none were of herself and Hugo.

Thank god Gloria has some kind of support network, Melissa thought, knowing what she planned to reveal.

Gloria returned with a tray of two mugs, an assortment of different teas, a pot of milk and some sugar. "Feel free to make your own tea, I've never known how people like it!"

Melissa laughed and observed Gloria as she sat down.

Despite her questionable fashion sense, especially for a biologist, Gloria looked completely different in her plain pyjamas; more approachable.

"Now, what's wrong, honey?" Gloria finally asked from across the room.

Melissa avoided Gloria's gaze from embarrassment, but she couldn't stop the tears from swamping her face.

Gloria hurried to her side and engulfed her into a tight hug.

"Oh, honey, you're such as mess! If you don't tell me what's wrong, I may not be able to let you leave this flat at all," Gloria joked.

But after the entrapment Melissa had faced from Andres *and* Hugo, her stomach twisted with dread, and she worried she had trusted the wrong person. What if Gloria had been working with Hugo all along as an accomplice?

Melissa searched Gloria's dark eyes, but all she saw was warmth and honesty.

"I got fired today," Melissa revealed, sniffling the tears away.

"Oh," Gloria murmured, raising her defined eyebrows. "Problems with the boss I see. What did the *cabron* do to you? He didn't try to feel you up, did he?"

"Actually, he didn't do anything. It's more of what I did to him."

Gloria nodded thoughtfully. "I see."

Melissa inhaled and looked into Gloria's eyes. "It's what *Hugo* did to him *because* of me, but before I go into that, I need to tell you the whole story."

Melissa lowered her head and her body trembled with shame.

She didn't want to lose Gloria's friendship, but coming clean seemed to be the only way to save it. All the lies had already troubled her mind enough to make her feel sick all the time and affect her appetite, and Hugo making a scene in her office had been the last straw.

"Tell me then, I'm all ears," Gloria encouraged with a soft smile.

Gloria reclined and caressed Melissa's thigh with her light touch.

Melissa expected to feel uncomfortable due to never being so close or intimate with another woman, but her muscles relaxed with ease.

"My boss asked me out today and Hugo saw the whole thing, so he went crazy on him and sent him flying," Melissa explained. "As a result, he fired me."

"Maybe Hugo was simply trying to honour his late brother and found you disrespectful? I mean, it's still quite early to be dating, if you don't mind me saying."

Melissa raised her eyebrows with surprise and Gloria noticed.

"What?" Gloria asked, grinning. "My family are very old-fashioned in that sense, and we require the proper amount of time to grieve, especially after losing a spouse."

Melissa nodded, but she didn't feel like sharing the horrors of her marriage. Besides, even she knew it was inappropriate to speak ill of the dead.

"I feel the same, so I didn't consider going out with him, but Hugo didn't give me the chance to explain before he emerged and punched him."

Gloria dipped her eyebrows. "Oh, that doesn't sound like Hugo at all. He is usually very thorough and a great listener."

A hint of jealousy stabbed Melissa in the heart; why couldn't Hugo have been so loving towards *her?*

"Well, I'm sure that's the case with *you*, but in my case, he jumped the guns and dragged me out of the office, telling Jason I wouldn't be back in the office anymore."

"Oh, so your boss didn't fire you? Hugo did?"

Melissa nodded without realising the incongruousness of her words. "Yes, he keeps telling me I need to pay him back for clearing my father's debts or…"

"Or what, honey?" Gloria prompted, brushing a loose strand of Melissa's hair behind her ear.

Melissa's body stiffened as she prepared for the blow she was about to land on Gloria.

She jerked her head up and breathed deep. "Or I should marry him and give him a child."

Gloria burst into laughter and placed her hand on Melissa's back. "I'm sorry, I don't mean to laugh at your despair, but Hugo makes me laugh. God, he is such an *alfa male* and *thick* sometimes."

"You're not upset at all?" Melissa asked in disbelief.

"Well, I'm certainly *disappointed,* and I will have a word with that insane man later to let him know that's not the way to treat a lady."

Melissa raised her eyebrows. "I feared you wouldn't let me explain and would blame me for his poor behaviour towards you."

Gloria's smile faded and her features hardened. "What do you mean towards me?"

Melissa eyed her like she had lost her mind. "Well, insisting on having a baby with me, even though you two are together?"

"Wow, time out, please. *What?*" Gloria exclaimed.

Melissa frowned. "I just told you that your *boyfriend* insisted on marrying me today, doesn't that make you upset at all?"

Gloria guffawed again. "Oh, trust me, my partner would not live to see the next day after proposing something like that to another girl, but Hugo and I have never been together. I'm not interested in the male gender like that."

Melissa stared at Gloria with a blank expression. "What do you mean?"

Gloria stood and giggled. "Melissa, look around you, what do you see?"

Melissa scanned the room and focused on the paintings and photographs dotted around. An enormous painting of a naked woman's body covered the wall opposite the sofa, and many framed photos pictured another woman in Gloria's embrace.

"Oh," Melissa said, realising the situation.

"Oh, indeed," Gloria said, sitting back down beside her.

"So, you were never with Hugo?"

Gloria shook her head.

"But why did you pretend such a thing? And don't tell me you didn't because I saw you both when you visited the mansion for the first time."

Gloria hesitated for a second. "Because Hugo asked me to pretend."

"What? Why?" Melissa exclaimed.

"I think it's better if he explains it to you," Gloria said, but Melissa grabbed her hand.

"Please don't call him, I need time! I don't want to see him right now," she begged.

Gloria stroked her crown. "I'm sorry, *cariño*, but I think he is here already."

Just then, the doorbell sounded, and Melissa jumped to her feet.

"I can't believe you called him!"

"I didn't, but you stole his car that has GPS, so he's obviously traced you here," Gloria said with a smirk on her face. "You should really check those things before trying to escape from your boyfriend."

"What do you mean?" Melissa yelled, but Gloria opened the door and Hugo stepped inside. "Laters, children. Behave yourselves, please!"

Gloria grinned at Melissa and shot a murderous look at Hugo before she left.

Hugo strode towards her, and Melissa cowered in the farthest corner. "Don't come any closer! You can talk from afar, I'll listen."

Hugo froze and raised his hands in surrender. "May I sit on the corner of the sofa at least? I won't try to touch you, I promise."

Melissa nodded and looked at him for the first time.

Dark circles surrounded his eyes and his red knuckles looked sore. He had buttoned his shirt up wrong, and his black jeans hung low as if he dressed in a hurry.

"*Lizzy*, I have a confession to make."

Melissa's eyes filled with more tears, and she realised how much she missed her father. No one had really allowed her the time to grieve after he died, and everything had happened so fast.

"I've told you many times, please don't use the nickname my father gave to me! It feels like you're mocking me."

"How can I not use it?" Hugo questioned. "Especially as your father used it so many times when we talked about you in his kitchen."

Melissa furrowed her brow and glared at Hugo.

"What do you mean?"

Hugo rubbed his neck and shuffled his feet. "I used to see him every week before he died. It was me who helped him around the house, the garden being one of them if you noticed when you last visited."

Melissa processed the information, but nothing made sense to her.

"Why would you visit my dad every week? You didn't even know him!" Melissa barked.

"That's not entirely true. You see, when you left for university, I studied both abroad and in the UK, but since most of my classes were virtual anyway, it didn't matter where I studied," Hugo said, taking a deep breath. "I couldn't bear to stay at the Ferrero Mansion. It reminded me too much of my mum, so one day while looking for a place to study, I saw your father carrying heavy groceries with a bad back."

They both grinned at the memory of Melissa's father, and Hugo continued.

"Anyway, I helped him, and he offered for me to use his living room to study, and before I knew it, he asked me to crash in your old room."

"You're telling me you slept in my childhood bedroom around my things?" Melissa snorted.

Hugo blushed. "It's not one of my proudest moments, but yes."

Melissa nodded and waited for him to resume.

"It kind of became a weekly reoccurrence to us, and we ended up planting trees in his garden. Unlike my own father, yours displayed interest in my opinion… and in *me*."

"I heard you had your issues with your father," Melissa confirmed.

"Yeah, that's to say the least. He lost his will to live when my mum died," Hugo replied, his voice cracking. "Anyway, your father knew I had a thing for his sweet *Lizzy*."

"What does that mean?"

"It means your father saw me stalking you on your way home from the library several times. My mum apologised to him, which probably didn't make your parents' relationship any easier for them."

"I don't recall seeing your mum in my house, ever."

"You wouldn't, you weren't in when that happened, but that's not the point of my story."

"What is your point then?" Melissa asked, remaining in the corner.

"My point is – when my brother asked you to marry him, I hated him as he knew about my feelings for you since we were kids. That's why I came to your house to tell you to stay away from him, but you still went and married him anyway."

The raw pain in his eyes tugged at Melissa's heart and she stepped a little closer to him. "I had no idea."

"You wouldn't have, and to be honest, I thought horrible things about you when I first heard that you had married Andres."

Melissa nodded. "I assume Gloria's role was meant to be some kind of statement to me every time you visited us?"

"Was it that obvious?" Hugo asked through a cheeky grin, exposing his white teeth.

Melissa shook her head. "No, especially as she's so gorgeous."

Hugo tilted his head, indecisive. "You could say so, but for me, she's got too much masculine energy, so much so that I sometimes felt interior to her."

Melissa laughed. "Trust me, I had my first glance today when I came here, and I will never doubt it again."

Hugo buried his face into his palms. "My god, I have been such as idiot, haven't I?"

"Well, I guess both of us are to blame somehow," Melissa said. "I feel really guilty about accepting your brother's proposal, and then falling for you despite what you did to him."

Hugo raised his hand in the air. "I'll come back to the falling bit in a minute, but first, what *I* did to him?"

"It's ok, Hugo, I don't blame you, these things can happen no matter what. Please let me be part of your secret," she reassured.

Hugo scratched his head. "Please let *me* be part of my secret as well. What did I do to my brother?"

"Well, you know, drink-driving when you picked up him and his friends from a party that caused him to lose his mobility," Melissa reminded, but Hugo stepped closed and took her hand.

"*Lizzy*, I wasn't drunk when I picked them up. They were high on cocaine, and to avoid the police catching them, I promised to rescue them. I was probably sleep-deprived, yeah, but I've always been a skilful driver. It was another drunk driver who came out of nowhere and hit us, but that wasn't my fault. That's what the insurance company even declared after their investigation."

Melissa gasped. "What?"

Hugo nodded. "Absolutely, I can show you the investigation report if you want, but that's what happened. I was just trying to protect my family."

A shadow descended over Melissa's face, and she pulled her hand away. "Yes, I remember, that's what you said when Andres told you to sleep with me to ensure that I don't ruin the family name."

Hugo averted his eyes and blushed. "I know that looks really bad on me, but he threatened to call one of his old buddies to do it for him if I didn't do it, and call me crazy, but I thought I would be the lesser of the two evils. I planned to simply entertain you without anything physical, but I couldn't resist the desire in your eyes. I wouldn't have lived without it."

Hugo closed the gap between them and smiled through the pain.

"Melissa, I know there are a lot of things we need to talk about, but trust me, no one will ever love you the way I do. I want to spend the rest of my life with you and replace all the sad memories with happy ones. Please, let me love you."

Pure joy filled Melissa's body and the air around them turned electric. Melissa beamed, but Hugo turned away.

"I understand if you don't want to," Hugo added, looking at the floor.

Melissa rolled her eyes with amusement and lifted his chin with her hand. She leaned in and pressed her lips against his, eliminating any doubt between them. Hugo caressed Melissa's body, and a lone tear trickled down his cheek.

The two of them parted and Melissa smiled.

"I love you too, Hugo Ferrero. Always have and always will."

EPILOGUE

Melissa woke up to her stomach twisting. She dragged herself out of bed, but the room immediately started spinning.

"*Amor mio*, are you ok?" Hugo asked and pulled her back to bed. "Careful, or you'll fall."

Melissa touched her clammy forehead and closed her eyes again. "I'm not sure. I think I ate something last night that made me feel sick all night. I barely closed my eyes."

Hugo narrowed his eyes. "Are you sure? Maybe it's just the day that makes you nervous?"

Hugo made a good point, considering that today was the day of Andres's funeral. The day both have dreaded.

"You might be right. I do feel a little nervous about people's reactions. Do you think they will notice that we are together now?"

Hugo shrugged and placed two fluffy pillows behind Melissa's back. "I don't really care. It's not people's business what happens in my life. If they want to talk, so be it. As long as they talk behind my back. I don't want anything to stress my beautiful woman."

Melissa blushed. "I just think we should keep our distance today. You know, out of respect."

"I don't think so," Hugo said and placed a passionate kiss on her lips.

"Hugo, I'm serious! The last thing I need is Mrs Whittle giving me her evil eye all afternoon. Despite my difficult relationship with your brother, I still want to end my marriage with him respectfully."

"And I admire you for that, *amor mio*," Hugo said and sighed. "OK, I will keep my hands to myself during the service, but we will both sit in the same row. After all, we are family, but that's the best I can do."

"Ok, then," Melissa said and relaxed against the pillows.

"How do you feel?"

"Slightly better. The nausea comes and goes."

Hugo eyed her knowingly. "We better get you a pregnancy test."

Melissa closed her eyes and touched her temples. "Please don't, I can't handle anything else right now."

"You don't have to. I'll pop into the pharmacy before the funeral and buy you one."

"I hope you don't make me do one at the funeral," Melissa joked.

"Where are your manners, Mrs Ferrero? Of course, we will leave the funeral and use one of the public toilets on the way home."

Melissa glared at him. "You better be joking."

Hugo grinned. "I might be."

"Let's just first get through this day and think about that again tomorrow. I'm sure it's nothing," Melissa said and climbed from the bed again. When Hugo followed her, she raised her hand. "No, my love, I'll shower alone this time."

Hugo's face fell. "Don't be ridiculous. One day of celibacy won't undo our relationship."

"It might not, but I don't feel like making myself feel worse than I already do."

Until You See Me

She didn't wait for Hugo's protest and closed the bathroom door.

***

"Are you ready to go?"

Melissa glanced at the door. "Yes, give me two minutes and I'll meet you at the door."

Hugo had showered in the guest room en-suite and dressed in a black suit. He had combed his hair back and shaved his beard. On his freshly shaven jawline, Melissa could see a tiny, fresh cut that told Melissa that he was nervous too.

Hugo nodded and disappeared from the doorway.

Melissa applied her signature red lipstick and let her hair down. She had chosen the simple black dress and pumps she had worn for Patrick's funeral; it gave her a sense of closure to end her relationship in the same way she had met Andres.

"You look gorgeous."

Melissa smiled. "Thank you, Hugo."

Hugo walked to her and lifted her jaw to face him. "What's wrong, *amor mio*. Why so sad?"

"I'm burying my husband and sleeping with his brother. I'm going straight to hell."

A lonely, melancholic tear emerge from the corner of her eye, and she buried her soft sobs into Hugo's chest.

"Shhh, I know. This is a difficult day."

"If it's difficult for me, I can only imagine what you must be going through right now," Melissa said and gazed at Hugo. "How are you holding up?"

Hugo raised his eyebrows, surprised. "I'm ok."

"And...?" Melissa prompted.

"Well, it's horrible to say this, but I kind of lost my brother years ago. We were never close, and we always had this ridiculous sibling rivalry going on that he took to the extreme..."

Hugo's voice cracked and Melissa hurried to console him. "It's ok, my love. I get it. I have never been close to my mum, but I still care about her a lot. It's ok not to *miss* them the same way you would miss someone close to you."

Hugo nodded and swallowed hard. "Shall we?"

Melissa nodded and stepped out of the door. They walked hand in hand to the car and Hugo kept the door open for her. She slipped into the passenger side and he sat behind the steering wheel.

"Did you speak to Jason?"

Melissa glanced at Hugo. "I did. He sends his greetings to you."

Hugo blushed. "I hope he won't sue me."

"He should though."

Hugo glared at Melissa. "Something tells me that you want me to learn my lesson."

"Definitely, you can't go around punching people like that."

"I was defending your honour against your boss."

"Well, you can try again with my new boss, I'm sure she will be thrilled at your efforts."

Hugo grinned. "How are you finding the new working environment with Gloria?

Melissa grew serious. "Well, even though Jason didn't mention your little fist fight again, I didn't feel comfortable going back there, so luckily, Gloria ran to the rescue with her offer of taking over Garcia Enterprises' accounts."

"Did I mention that I was sorry?"

"Too little too late, Hugo, but it's ok. I like working with her. Besides I can still see my old colleagues when going through the accounts with them."

"And you can work from home as well. We can convert one of the guest rooms into your office," Hugo said and parked the car at Fulham Cemetery in West London.

He helped Melissa out, and together, they walked with the pastor to the small chapel up at the hill. The moment they entered, the first drops of rain hit the ground.

Poetic, Melissa thought.

The chapel was decorated with white roses, and candles circulated the black coffin. Melissa was surprised to find the chapel nearly empty, apart from a few members of family and friends. Mrs Whittle sat in the first row and sobbed loudly. Hugo approached her and engulfed the old lady into a bear hug.

"Oh, master Hugo, what are we going to do now?"

Hugo hugged the old lady tightly. "I don't know, Grace. I don't know."

Melissa stood behind Hugo and let them have their moment. She was surprised they were on a first-name basis as she had never heard Mrs Whittle refer to Andres by his first name.

Suddenly Hugo moved and said, "Do you remember Mrs Ferrero?"

Melissa froze, but after seeing Mrs Whittle's tired eyes full of tears, she extended both her arms. "Just call me Melissa. I'm so sorry for your loss. I know Andres was like a son to you."

"Thank you, Melissa, I'm sorry too," Mrs Whittle said, and for some reason, Melissa felt that she wasn't apologising only for losing Andres.

After the short ceremony, everyone walked to the Ferrero mausoleum on the West side of the cemetery, the rain a little heavier than before, but the pastor kindly lent everyone umbrellas to cover themselves from the downpour. Melissa let Hugo take his time saying his final goodbyes to his twin brother and they both left in silence.

Melissa still couldn't believe the demanding, gorgeous man who had entered her life and taken it by storm.

It must be fate, she thought as she entered a public toilet on the way home, a pregnancy test in her hand.

"Well?" Hugo asked upon her return, standing up and raising his brow.

"Praise yourself, Mr Ferrero. You're going to be a father."

***

"Hugo, do you want to talk about this?" Melissa asked, placing the takeaway order on the kitchen counter.

After she had broken the news to him, he had barricaded himself into his home office. Only the smell of his favourite spicy takeaway curry could lure him out.

"Hmm…" Hugo nodded and searched the take-away bags.

"I mean, this was hardly something neither of us expected, so I completely understand if you are not comfortable with the idea of being a father."

Hugo dropped the bags on the counter. "And what is that supposed to mean?"

Melissa shrugged. "Nothing. If you don't want to be in our lives, I get it, but just so you know, I will do it alone."

"Absolutely not!" Hugo yelled.

"Then what is your problem?" Melissa huffed.

She understood that the news was a surprise to Hugo, but she had just learnt it as well and had a hard time digesting the new information.

"Nothing, it's just new to me. I never imagined myself as a father and I had such a poor example growing up, I'm not sure how to deal with this."

Melissa's heart melted. She walked around the counter and embraced him from behind. "I know, my love, it's a new situation for me as well, but we will learn together. Every mistake your father made, you can replace with different behaviour."

Hugo sighed and kissed Melissa's crown. "You might be right, *amor mio*. What would I do without you?"

***

The next day, Hugo booked an appointment with his family doctor to confirm the pregnancy. Although, there was very little to be confirmed as Melissa's morning sickness was more than enough proof.

They arrived at the West London clinic and Hugo parked in VIP parking.

"Is there anything the Ferrero family does low-key?" Melissa asked.

Hugo's mouth twitched. "This is low-key. You see, no one around."

Melissa huffed and got out of the car. The mood swings had come with the morning sickness.

"*Por dios, mujer,* can you please wait for me to open the door for you?" Hugo complained and hurried to open the clinic door for Melissa.

"Hugo, I'm not sick. I'm probably pregnant. I can open my own doors."

Until You See Me

"Probably? You're either pregnant or bipolar," Hugo said and walked to the reception desk to check in.

Melissa poked her tongue out at Hugo's back, satisfying her as all the hormones raged around her body.

"Mr and Mrs Ferrero?" the doctor called.

They both stood up and walked hand in hand to the small consulting room.

"What do we have here today?"

"It looks like Melissa is pregnant," Hugo blurted.

"That's wonderful news!" the doctor exclaimed and clapped his hands together.

Melissa smiled. He reminded her of her father.

"Can we please confirm the pregnancy, doctor?" Hugo asked impatiently.

"Sure, we just need you to do a urine sample and a blood test as it will give the most accurate result, especially if you're not far off. We won't be listening to any heartbeats as they are only noticeable from week seven, but some women need to wait until week twelve to hear anything. I just want to manage your expectations."

Melissa nodded as Hugo helped her to the treatment chair and held her hand during the blood test.

"This will take an hour or two, but let's see what the urine sample tells us," the doctor said and handed the small cup to Melissa. When Hugo stood up, Melissa raised her finger. "No, you will definitely not accompany me to the toilet! Are you crazy?"

Hugo sat down slowly and let Melissa go.

It didn't take her long to complete the test and wrap it into a brown paper bag, which she left at the nurse's station and returned to the consulting room.

They waited silently for the doctor to come back.

"Well, congratulations are in order, you are pregnant." The doctor smiled. "And it looks like you're farther along than expected, so we can do an ultrasound scan if you both want?"

Melissa froze. "What does that mean?"

"It means you have fallen pregnant earlier than anticipated, but don't worry, if we do an ultrasound scan, I can tell you a lot more," the doctor reassured.

Melissa sensed the shift in Hugo's mood.

What on earth could it be this time? she thought, but focused on the doctor again.

"Hmm, it looks like you are already on your fourth month, Melissa. I would say week fourteen to be exact."

"Week fourteen!?" Hugo cried.

Melissa tensed. "How can that be possible, Doctor? How could I not notice it before?"

The doctor shook his head. "There can be many reasons. Obviously, I don't have to go through the process of *how* you fell pregnant..." he said, eying them both through his glasses. "... but many women bleed during their first few months of pregnancy and mistake it for a period rather than implantation."

"Is the baby ok? Can we hear the heartbeat?" Hugo asked.

The old doctor smiled. "The baby is fine, I'm just trying to find a clear heartbeat, but it sounds like..."

"Like what, Doctor?" Hugo prompted.

"Well, it seems that... let me see the scan again," he said, and both Melissa and Hugo tensed. Melissa's hand searched for Hugo's, and together, they looked at the doctor expectantly.

"It seems you have been double blessed. I can hear two heartbeats and see two fetuses. You are expecting twins."

"Oh my goodness."

"This shouldn't be a surprise to you both as Hugo is a twin," the doctor reminded and pulled his chair back to let Melissa readjust her clothes.

Melissa remained quiet for the rest of the scan and only nodded when Hugo asked specifying questions. On their way down to the car park, Hugo opened his mouth again.

"Did you have sex with Andres?" he blurted.

"What?! How dare you ask me this!"

"Just answer the simple question."

"If you must know, no I didn't. So, this is your mess from our first night."

Hugo nodded. "That's what I thought, but worth checking. Anyway, you know I would have loved the kids like my own no matter what."

"Right." Melissa pouted and silence fell in the car.

When they got home, Melissa tried to leave the car when Hugo grabbed her hand. "For what it's worth, I'm sorry for being a jerk. It's just a lot of adjusting, but I couldn't be happier."

Melissa turned to look at him. "Are you sure? You have seemed so moody lately."

Hugo embraced her and planted a kiss on her forehead. "I'm sure, *mi vida*. This is the happiest day of my life. Hearing that we have been blessed not only with one kid but two means the world to me."

Melissa smiled. "Then we are on the same page."

"Good, then I guess there is only one thing to do..."

Melissa raised her eyebrows. "Okay?"

"Follow me," Hugo said and opened the car door.

"Why is it all dark in the car park?" she asked and took a couple of unsteady steps when a pool of candles lit around her. "Oh my God. What is this?"

"Just follow the trail," Hugo said and took her hand into his.

They ambled towards the private lift that led to Hugo's home, and when they reached the penthouse, Melissa could see the lit candle trail continue to the front door with red and white rose petals. Hugo opened the door and they both stepped inside.

Melissa eyed the white interior that seemed untouched. "Good. For a second I was worried about the fire safety if you left the candles alone at the flat."

"It's not over yet," Hugo said and led the way to the balcony.

When Melissa stepped inside, she couldn't believe her eyes. The balcony had been transformed into an ocean of flowers and candles, and in the middle of them, there were two chairs and a table enveloped in fresh white table wear.

Hugo took the bottle from the ice and opened it, but before Melissa had the chance to protest, he turned the bottle around and said, "Non-alcoholic. Don't worry."

"How did you know?" Melissa asked, surprised.

"Let's just say I had a good hunch."

Hugo winked and poured two tall glasses of bubbly liquid. Melissa sipped the drink and savoured the taste in her mouth. "This is what I needed after today. Regardless of whether it's alcoholic or not."

Hugo smiled and prompted her to sit down. "I'm glad you like it. Your mother helped me to organise everything."

Melissa's eyes bulged. "My mother?"

"Yes." Hugo nodded. "Especially as I told her of the occasion…"

Melissa frowned. "What occasion?"

Hugo pulled out a small velvet box from his pocket.

Melissa froze. "What is it?"

"It's a different type of proposal."

"I hope you do a better job than the last time," Melissa teased, and for the first time in her life, she saw Hugo blush.

"I didn't do that good a job then, did I?"

Melissa shook her head.

"Ok then, let me try again…" he said and cleared his throat. "Melissa, for as long as I've known you, I've always been fascinated by you. There has been something in you that reflected peace and calmness, which I always craved in this life. I need you to be my safe haven during the storms and the anchor when I feel lost. I know I almost ruined it all, but here I am on my knee…to ask you to be my wife. Will you marry me?"

"Oh my God…" Melissa gasped.

On some level, she knew it had been coming, but she hadn't expected it on the day of his brother's funeral.

Melissa stepped closer to him and sank to her knees in front of him. "Isn't it too soon, Hugo? I mean we have a lifetime together…"

Hugo shook his head hard. "I can't go on a minute longer without having you as my wife. I dreamt of this moment for such a long time without realising it, so I won't rest until you have my ring on your finger to remind you that you belong to me. Until you finally see me."

Melissa felt a lump in her throat, but her heart was full of joy.

For the first time in her life, she felt completely at peace after the storm.

She caressed Hugo's jawline and lifted his gaze. "I would be honoured to be your wife, Hugo. Nothing would make me happier, and I'm so happy that you finally see me too."

Printed in Great Britain
by Amazon